LIFE GETS IN THE WAY

Jerry Baggett

LIFE GETS IN THE WAY

A McGowin Thriller

Vanguard Press

VANGUARD PAPERBACK

© Copyright 2022
Jerry Baggett

A CIP catalogue record for this title is available from the British
Library.
ISBN 978-1-80016-452-9

This is a work of fiction. Names, characters, businesses, places,
events and incidents are either the products of the author's
imagination or used in a fictitious manner. Any resemblance to
actual persons, living or dead, or actual events is purely
coincidental.

Vanguard Press is an imprint of
Pegasus Elliot Mackenzie Publishers Ltd.
www.pegasuspublishers.com

First Published in 2022

Vanguard Press
Sheraton House Castle Park
Cambridge England

Printed & Bound in Great Britain

Author's note

To my readers
Life Gets in The Way is a revised second edition
of Oceans Apart.

Dedicated to
Digby, Bob, and Johnny
Warriors all
and the families who loved them

*"If we are to guard against ignorance
And remain free, it is the responsibility
of every American to be informed."*

Thomas Jefferson

Chapter 1

Mike McGowin eased *Blue Dolphin* into the calm anchorage on the lee side of the small island an hour after sunset. He entered a final note in the ship's log. The fourteen-hundred-mile trip had taken seventy-eight hours. Their only stop, La Paz, Mexico to pick up family members.

The entire vessel buzzed with activity. He set the ship's GPS anchor safety alarm, checked all power systems and picked up high-resolution binoculars to look over the beach. Visibility was excellent in the bright moonlight. A small boat with an outboard motor had been dragged onto shore a short distance down the beach. He saw no human activity anywhere within his viewing area. He looked forward to a beer and hurried out to join the ship's crew enjoying happy hour on the sun-deck

Mike rose early. He glanced out at the first rays of dawn reflecting off a glassy sea and eased forward into the galley to coax a cup of bold coffee from the single cup machine. Something passing by outside caught his eye through the galley port-hole. He leaned down for a better look. A shadow, no! A small boat, with several men inside. *Damn! Of all the luck.* He dropped his cup on the table and ran up through the main salon knowing entrance to *Blue Dolphin* would have to be made through there with men entering from the cockpit. Three ragged looking men sat comfortably with guns pointed at him.

The heavily bearded man in a battered straw hat eased to his feet. "Relax, Captain." He waved his hand in a dismissive gesture. "I'm going to tell you what we want from you and you will do exactly as you're told. Understand?"

Mike didn't allow himself to visibly react. "I presume you are the leader of these men. You all have weapons. Now tell me what it'll take to leave us alone. We have women and children on board. I can't jeopardize their safety."

"We're just poor, honest fishermen. You and your fancy yacht are in our fishing grounds depriving us of our livelihood. You will go below and gather all the valuables from your men and women. That includes all the cash, any watches, jewelry, wedding rings and especially expensive diamond rings on the fingers of your women. Listen carefully." He looked directly into Mike's eyes. "If one woman or child attempts to hide anything at all I will sever one or more fingers from their right hand. The number of fingers depends on how irritated I become over the incident." He inched closer. "Do you have a clear understanding of what I'm telling you?"

Mike nodded. "What guarantee do I have that you'll leave us alone after you have everything of value?" He backed away a step waiting for an answer. "You are not of Mexican nationality like your associates," he said. "Your English is perfectly spoken."

"And you are asking for a bullet in the gut, big man. I might add, any attempt to reach the radio will get all on board killed. We'll burn your fancy boat to the waterline. Now, stop wasting my time. We know precisely how many people are on board and that includes the children. If anyone appears with a weapon of any kind, everyone here will die. If you believe the Mexican authorities will save you, then you are wrong. The patrol boat for this area has moved south for the next four days. A call on the radio will only get you in trouble. Your vessel will be searched, and you will be taken into port for days of paperwork and questioning. Hector will escort you below. He will hold the gun on you while you enter each room and return with the valuables, cell phones first in each case."

Mike watched three more rag tag men come down from the upper deck. *How in hell did they get aboard so quietly?*

"These men will stand guard outside each room while you and Hector enter. Remember to do what you're told, and we will not embarrass or molest your women. Give me any reason at all and some will die, possibly all of you." He looked at his watch. "You have ten minutes to finish the job. Now go."

Mike turned and moved four steps to his left. He looked the bearded man in the eyes. "The word of one civilized man to another. There will be no trouble. What I'm offering is far more valuable to you than the few trinkets of assorted personal items and the risk to you will be far less. Please take what I offer and go quietly without awaking my crew."

Mike kneeled and punched in a combination below the hinged chart table.

"The ship's emergency cash is kept here. I believe this will satisfy you and your men. Allow me to lift out the locked cash box."

The two men stared at one another. Neither spoke for several moments. He felt they understood each other.

Mike reached inside the cabinet, lifted out the heavy metal box with both hands and passed it to the pirate. "I have the second combination. It's yours if you give me your word and leave before my crew wakes and starts moving about."

The pirate said, "Let me see what you have to offer."

Mike reached for the heavy box. He punched in the code and handed it back.

The man looked at the contents of the open box, then back at Mike. "How much is here? Don't lie to me."

"At least fourteen thousand dollars, maybe more. Count it if you wish."

The pirate put his hand inside, pushed his fingers deep and pulled out several bound packs of fifty-dollar bills.

Mike watched the panga pull away. He yelled. "Joel! Are you OK?" He'd started worrying about Joel as soon as the three men came down from the top deck. *Please be all right*, he thought. "Joel, answer me!" He bounded up the ladder.

Joel sat with his mouth taped over. His hands and feet were tied. Mike ripped the tape away, then pulled the wad of paper towels out of Joel's mouth. "What happened?"

Joel nodded his head to one side, looking in that direction. "Look out there, Mike. Our guests are fighting over the loot."

Mike watched the small gang of rag-tag fishermen in a beat-to-pieces wooden boat with a small outboard motor fight over the prize money. Several shots were fired.

Chapter 2

Mike dropped below and returned with a nine-millimeter Glock in his belt. "Let's see how it plays out with these guys. Dad called that packet of bills his insurance policy. I never expected to use it. It's preferable to my own insurance here that should have been close at hand."

Joel grinned. "I wondered how you would handle this situation, Mike."

They watched while five of the eight pirates took the lion's share of the spoils after an argument between themselves. Two men attacked the leader. He opened fire, killing two more, leaving another body drifting away in the light swell. *Only one or two will end up with the loot,* Mike thought.

"Joel, I believe we're ready for a new dive spot. That shot's going to wake the sleeping crew. Someone will rush up with questions we'd rather not answer."

Barbara came up from the galley where she'd started the large coffee maker, preparing for a morning meal. She and her husband owned a small waterside restaurant in the marina until he died accidentally while night diving for lobster.

Now, she managed the household for Marcus McGowin. "The sun's barely peeping up out of the Sea of Cortez, she said. "You guys have been making too much noise up here. You could wake the dead. What the heck's going on? That sounded like shooting."

Mike reached for the coffee she offered with one hand and grabbed the microphone for the ship to shore radio with the other. "Look off on the starboard side, toward the island, Barbara. There's a body floating in the water there."

"You missed all the excitement," Joel said. "A panga load of fishermen started fighting each other. Their friends took off in another boat. They left one in the water and two more lying dead in the panga. We're leaving for another island, someplace farther away from the mainland."

Mike placed the microphone back on the hook. "I reported the incident to the Mexican coastguard. They didn't seem very happy, but will have a helicopter cruise over the area looking for the men." He caught Joel's eye. "Step up topside for a few things Joel. After that we'll pull the anchor and move on to a better dive spot."

They looked over the small island, then back out to sea. Their visitors had moved on.

Mike nodded. "Thanks for covering things, Joel. We can't have the family upset. My sisters would grab the kids and return to California, ruining a perfectly good vacation. We'll be more careful from now on."

Barbara returned again from her galley duty. "What's going on? You guys are plotting something. Life can't get any better than this. So don't tell me we're leaving again."

Mike tapped her arm. "We feel it would be best to move on to another small island for diving and using the water toys. There's too much activity from local fishermen around here."

"Okay then," Barbara said. "Enjoy the quiet while you can. The kids are going to be out early."

He noticed a tray loaded with Bloody Mary fixings, untouched, but tempting.

Barbara said, "Omelets for the adults, walnut pancakes for the kids in one hour."

Mike carefully studied the depth of the chosen dive site. A thin veil of morning haze blocked some of brilliance from the morning sun emerging out of the Sea of Cortez. "It's going to be hot out once the overcast dissipates."

Joel wiped his brow. "You got that right. I'm heading down to throw out some snorkel gear."

The young crew rushed to the railing and looked down into magnificently clear water, mesmerized by a variety of active sea life milling about over the white sandy bottom.

"Open up all the doors, latch them back," Phil said. "That goes for several port holes below. The dry, light breeze is perfect inside or out. We can do without the air conditioning for a while."

The ship's power generators, designed with a dry stack exhaust system, vented the pre-cooled, muffled exhaust quietly out through the hollow superstructure. The design prevented exposing swimmers in the water to the generators' deadly exhaust gasses.

Brett led the team of snorkelers to the dive compartment. They dragged out dive bags for the young people, eager to grab snorkel equipment and enter the warm water.

Several large dive bags were left scattered around the cockpit for adults to pick up.

Sally, the thirty-eight-year-old, chief financial officer for the McGowin company and husband Phil had one son and one daughter, Bret and Samantha.

Gayle, forty-three, Mike's other sister, was president of the family-owned company. She and husband Robert had one daughter, Tanya.

Sally pointed. "Look at that." A curious trio of dolphin had moved in to investigate the strange activity.

Tanya, already in the water, screamed with delight. "That one came close enough for me to slide my fingers along her slippery side. Mom, you should see all the fish down there."

The adults toasted the great weather with their first cocktail of the day.

Smiling, Sally nudged Joel. "Activate the com system, please. We can spy on that wild activity in the water below."

The sensitive microphones for this system were placed strategically throughout the vessel. Voices could be passed to the bridge speakers, or other specific points inside or outside the vessel.

The day flashed by quickly with the kids playing on wet bikes and the adults water skiing. After a lunch break and afternoon rest, the activity started up all over again with the sun dipping low into the Sea of Cortez, Joel flipped a few switches in the console above the helm. The sound of madcap activity emerged from a recessed speaker beneath the lip of the superstructure. He triggered another switch and bright underwater lights illuminated the darkening water beneath and around *Blue Dolphin.*

The kids in the water appeared shocked to see the sudden reflection of bright light off a white sandy bottom. A variety of brightly colored sea life surrounded the snorkelers. An hour later Barb called everyone inside for the evening meal. "Have your meal first and then we'll attend those sunburned bodies. Tomorrow, we reapply sunscreen every hour."

Joel called out, "Hey, Mike, the divers are waiting for you. Water clarity is great this morning."

Mike left the sundeck to ready the tender for the morning dive. "Listen up, everyone, just for a minute. This is your first dive with tanks this trip. I know we've all been on many dives together, but just remember the basics. We're anchored in only forty feet of clear warm water. The visibility back from the surf in this anchorage should be excellent wherever you go. Remember: even on a shallow dive, follow behind your bubbles when returning to the surface. If you leave the bottom with your lungs full, slowly exhale on the way up."

He pointed at Sara. "You sometimes forget to keep your eye on your air pressure gauge and come up struggling for air, don't forget again. Always know your depth and the amount of air in your tank. Brett has more experience, so he should lead on this dive, with Samantha in the rear. Tanya, you and Sara spread out behind Brett."

He looked to see if they were paying attention. "Samantha, you have a new camera. Follow behind and around taking pictures, tail-o-the-fish, so to speak. Try to keep each other in sight. Now, if you see something to be checked out on the bottom it slows the dive, tap on your tank a few times with your dive knife, not the rapid danger signal, but slowly. Always respond to a tapping signal. Now, listen up, the big old sailboat beneath our vessel will be tempting to someone curious enough to enter. Don't. The top deck is about thirty feet deep, so you can look it over. However, never attempt to enter or reach inside any opening where an unexpected inhabitant might be located. Tap on the hull with your dive knife a few times. You might be surprised at what scoots out."

Mike swallowed some beer. "I'll be in the tender above following your bubbles. If there's any problem at all, surface slowly and I'll be there. You each have 2300 pounds of air. That should give you enough for a nice, swim over the bottom. I would like to see 500 pounds remaining, so I know you're watching your gauges. Any questions?"

He guided the tender over a steady stream of air-bubbles rising from the divers. They followed a small school of large colorful fish, always just out of their reach. He watched the scene below in crystal-clear water until his view became obstructed by their bubbles. After nearly an hour, he felt the hot sun, wanted a cold beer. Moments later he watched the dive leader pop to the surface.

Sara and Tanya chatted away about this one or that one followed through the shallow canyons.

Sara climbed over the short dive ladder laughing. She dropped her tank in the tender. "Some of those darn fish kept nibbling at my freckles."

Tanya yelled from the water, "Yeah! that big yellow one really liked you, Sara. I almost touched him a couple of times."

The next day, Mike made a scenic cruise around Isla San Jose. They approached the chosen anchorage at midday. Another small island, *Ideal for the water toys,* he thought. *We can spend one night here before our final dive at Espirito Santorito.*

Joel launched the two wet-bikes and the small tender for water skiing.

Near noon the next day Mike picked up the mike and announced loudly, "All lazy fat burners asleep in the sun, wake up. Look out at the beauty before you. That's Isla Espirito Santorito, the diving paradise you've all been waiting for."

Everyone moved to the starboard railing to get a look at the cove with crystal-clear water and a white sandy beach.

Gayle slapped Mike on the arm. "You did it again, fella, another great choice anchorage. Just look at those tiny waves hitting the beach. Just how deep is the water, Mike?"

"Only thirty-five feet, Gayle, maybe forty in some places. A young diver's paradise. He recalled diving here with his father at age fifteen. He put on an old beat-up wide brim straw hat and watched the divers suit up.

Eventually, after the divers were ready, he climbed aboard the tender. "Listen up, guys and gals. You may find this interesting. My dad dived with me here when I was fifteen years old. Once on the bottom you'll understand why the fishing is so good off this small island. I've measured all other fish habitats against this one for years. None ever replaced it as my favorite. Hope you will like it too. Expect a lot of narrow shallow canyons leading out away from the cove, all full of fish."

He followed over the divers with the tender. The bottom was mostly rocky, with enough white sand to reflect bright sunlight, making visibility excellent. Long shimmering sea grasses camouflaged the many varieties of colorful fish. Large manta rays swam over the bottom, seemingly unafraid of the divers and their constant cavalcade of air bubbles tumbling toward the surface. The ever-present sea lions were no longer afraid and came in close, evermore curious. A large bait ball spun toward the divers threatening to engulf them, only to spin away, shimmering in the bright sunlight. Some of the schooling fish were as long as a man's arm. Many with bright yellow tails swam close and nibbled at exposed flesh, not breaking the skin but still frightening. A pair of dolphins swam close to examine the divers. Some looked straight into the face plate of divers before swimming away.

Sara removed her dive mask, screaming at Mike. "This was the best dive ever, Mike. I can't wait to see our pictures on the big screen. Sam got an awesome picture of Brett riding a giant bat-ray. I also grabbed some great pictures of the big barracuda circling around looking for food."

She tossed her face plate and fins into the tender. "That one shot of Tanya coming out of the bait ball has to be the best ever."

A full week and two days just evaporated like dew in the morning sun. *Our last stop tomorrow, then the long haul back home.*

Sally yelled from above, "What would you say about putting into port at La Paz overnight?"

Mike yelled back, "Hey, that's up to you and Gayle. I'm always flexible with these things." He knew the fine Mexican restaurants were too tempting for his sisters. Today reminded him of why his dad loved the Baja area so much when he travelled here with his family.

Berthed on an outer mooring, *Blue Dolphin* provided a beautiful view into the bay of La Paz.

Mike stood on the foredeck drinking coffee with Barbara. "I know how you love preparing big meals, Barb. I've made seven o'clock reservations for everyone at Las Tres Vergennes restaurant across town. I can make it up to you by letting you prepare me a large chicken fried steak and egg breakfast tomorrow, if it'll make you feel better."

Barbara grabbed Mike's cap and yanked it down hard over his ears. "You just can't stay out of trouble, can you, big guy?"

Moments later, she returned, finding him on the bridge with Joel. She had the coffee thermos, refilled all three cups, left, then returned again with two large pieces of peach pie smothered with ice cream. She placed a much smaller piece on the table for herself. "We have two hours before leaving for dinner ashore. There's no use leaving tonight's dessert, is there?"

Joel said, "Barbara, you have to marry me. I'm spoiled already for anyone else. Mike, as captain of the ship, can't you perform the ceremony?"

"Yes, I can do that. However, the ceremony is only good for the duration of the cruise."

"Perfect! Then, how about it, Barbara?"

"No chance, Prince Charming. It's got to be a life sentence or none at all."

"Why haven't you married again, Barbara? You're still young and attractive."

"I don't know. Maybe I feel like Marcus McGowin. He said life only gets better when the last child leaves home and old Rover dies. I was never fortunate enough to have children. But life's good. Maybe I've reached that point."

Mike said, "Not so, Barbara. You just might turn around one day and feel that thrill of romance again. Look at the three of us sitting here, all single. Are any of you ready to give up the quest? I don't think so."

Chapter 3

Mike spread the navigation chart across the table. He stepped off his desired course and put away the protractor, jotting down a few notes on a pad. He looked up to see Joel reaching out with a cup of coffee. "The course is set for a straight shot back to San Diego, Joel. I've allowed for good coastal clearance, running twenty-four hours steady. The coastline of the Baha Peninsula runs approximately 335 degrees north-by-northwest. We'll have a straight six-hundred-mile run, slipping between Alijos Rocks and Rosa Banks. Then a straight shot outside Isla Cerros on a heading of 155 degrees. We can plug into the system and get ETA, fuel usage and a more accurate plot before shoving off."

Joel nodded. "*Blue Dolphin's* ready. I finished the engine room check this morning. Both generators have performed well, although the small twelve KW needs servicing. It's been running twenty-four hours a day for that damn water maker."

"With only two onboard, we shouldn't need to make more water for a week or so, pal. How about the cats? Have you noticed more high temperature on the port side?"

"No problem since I cleaned seaweed out of the saltwater intake filter. Those damn twelve-cylinder beasts don't miss a beat. We averaged nearly twenty knots at 2800 RPM down the sea of Cortez. Also, we took on an additional 2300 gallons of number two diesel fuel. With what we have on board that should leave some cheap fuel for use in the home waters."

"How about finishing up your chores, Joel, so we can go ashore for one last good Mexican dinner before leaving Cabo?"

"You're a gringo after my own heart, Mike. I know just the place. It's four or five miles from the marina so we'll have to grab a cab. There's some damn good Mexican food and the Mexican beer ain't bad either. It's always popular with expatriate Americans, and occasionally has a little dust up. If anybody picks on you, Mike, I'll whip his ass. After all, I did promise your old man I'd look after you down here."

Dressed in fishing shorts and T-shirt, Mike's six-foot four inch, two hundred forty-five-pound frame and muscular thighs left the outer seams of his fishing shorts ripped near the bottom. His muscular torso stressed the well-worn T-shirt.

"Why you little shit, Joel. You couldn't weigh more than a buck-sixty. But you do remind me of a firmly packed watch-it."

"What the hell is a watch-it?"

"A watch-it, my cocky friend, is ten pounds of horseshit in a five-pound bag. If one comes your way, you'd better watch it." *He's a tough little shit, a few small scars around his eyes and mouth from his golden glove fights.*

"Aw, come on now. You really mean two-hundred-pounds of tiger packed into a hundred-sixty-pound body."

After a fifteen-minute taxi ride, the two friends entered a decent looking, moderately busy restaurant. Joel pointed to a table near the dance floor where people were leaving. "There's an open table."

"Let's get farther away from the loud music, maybe that booth in the center rear. It's open."

The booth was small, intended for four people. Mike shoved the table closer to Joel's side and sat down. "Most people at the bar are smoking, but so far, the smoke's not bad. It's clear to see why you like this place, pal. All the bar maids wear string bikinis. And look there, the food servers are well dressed, short white aprons over bikinis."

Joel said, "Order us up a couple of Cadillac margaritas while I hit the head."

Mike looked at the bar crowd. The place was no different than a hundred watering holes he'd parked his butt in around the world.

He watched a couple of "Blue Moons" working the bar. Beyond those girls, some tough looking men, drinking heavy. That table in the dimly lit corner had all the ingredients for trouble: two attractive gringo women, one gringo male and a couple of tough looking Mexican men. The two women attempted to leave. The big gringo yelled out, "Sit down, damn it!" He downed a shot of tequila, smirked, and pushed the blonde woman back down into her chair. The tall brunette slapped him hard across the face, a sound like a rifle shot. The man delivered a blow to the woman's temple that sent her to the floor out of sight. *Damn! I sure called that one,* he thought.

Standing, Mike said, "This is not our problem, Joel. Nevertheless, I hate bruisers who abuse women. It's time for a little retribution. Pay the check so we can get out of here on our own terms."

Throwing money on the table, Joel said, "You'd better get your attention on something besides that blonde over there. The cocktail girl said that big white guy and the Mexicans are known narco crowd."

Mike wanted a better look at that dark-haired girl. It was so damn dark in that corner. Only an occasional side view of a classic profile and full lips. That always got to him. He didn't understand women who put themselves in situations like that.

"You're going to get our asses in trouble, deep trouble. This's not our territory, Mike. We're all alone down here, and I don't like Mexican jails." He grabbed Mike's arm. "Wait. He's headed away from the others. Give him a sec, Okay? Take care of business, if you feel you must, while I offer my help to the ladies. Even if it gets my ass kicked."

Mike waited a few moments. He walked down a narrow, dim hallway toward the men's room. He listened at the door, heard water running, no conversation, and entered.

The woman beater grinned. Mike ignored the grin and moved to his right. The thug opened a long switch blade and lunged. Mike stepped up to his left and slammed his right foot into the man's exposed rib cage. Cracked ribs sounded like the earlier face slap. He knew several ribs were busted. The blow sent the man hard against the porcelain urinal. He collapsed to the dirty floor, gasping for breath. Mike reached down, picked up the knife, wedged the blade into a crack in the block wall, pressed down on the handle, snapping the blade off.

Grimacing in pain, the hoodlum growled at Mike. "You don't know who I am, asshole. You won't get out of here in one piece."

Mike looked into the man's eyes, grabbed his head with both hands and slammed his face hard against the piss covered floor, splattering piss and blood on the wall around the urinal. "The ribs are for the women you abused. The face is for the threat you just made to me."

He left the men's room. He didn't see the women. Then he saw the two Mexican men facing off with Joel. He headed towards them.

The big man with a mean look sent the two thugs away, past the bar and down another dim hallway toward the ladies' room. "Let's get the hell out of here, Joel. Trouble is on its way. That guy's in no condition to be chasing those women around now. They should be fine, but we may have a posse after us soon. Leaving Cabo San Lucas at zero dark thirty could be a good idea, pal."

"Oh yeah. It didn't take us long to get into trouble, did it?"

Mike and Joel walked to a small convenience store, spotted a cab and were dropped off within a mile of the Baha marina. They walked to the boat from there.

What the hell have I got us into now! "You know, Joel. We'll be terribly busy once we get back to Los Angeles. I have a corporate board meeting on the twenty-first that requires some prep work. Then we start the remodel on the Wilshire property. That means I'll be tied up through the rest of the year, and you, my friend, have five office buildings that you're responsible for. Regardless of that, something tells me that we should take our time about returning home, and try to get a few more good dives in, weather permitting of course. This way we'll be hiding in plain sight for a while."

"Okay, Mike. I think it'd be a mistake to take those narco guys too lightly. That guy back there'll be turning over every rock in sight trying to find us. If he connects us with the *Blue Dolphin*, our asses are worm food."

"You're absolutely right. You know, I've always wanted to dive Guadalupe Island. But it seemed so far away. Maybe a side trip now would be appropriate. It's on our way home and just might take us away from the action for a week or so."

He hesitated long enough to collect his thoughts. "The galley is loaded up and fuel's not a problem. Guadalupe is certainly off the beaten path. Few vessels have the range for a round trip out that far."

"That it is," Joel added. "This might be the best time for a visit. I can have all the dive tanks filled by the time we get there. We don't have a diver's guide for the island on board, do we?"

Chapter 4

The atmosphere close to the island was oppressive. Mike filleted the fleshy body and tossed the skeleton overboard. Their meal for this evening. *He hated sweat rolling down his back.*

"You know, Joel, I'm concerned. We left Cabo so fast after kicking hell out of that narco shit. We need some knowledge of what's going on. It's possible they picked up our trail. He's not likely to take a beating and just forget about it."

Joel took the pressure regulator off a dive tank and dropped it in fresh water. "Diverting to Guadalupe Island bought us a few days. We've had fun here but it's probably time to move our asses."

"Yeah, you haven't spotted that big sport fisher again, the one that passed south of us a few days ago?"

Joel shook his head. "The more reason to grab the hook and get the hell out of Mexico. Those guys avoided close contact with us for a reason."

"I agree. It's better to be safe than sorry. The weather report looks decent for the next few days. We'd better be underway before dawn."

"Sound's good. We'll buck a fifteen-knot head wind after a couple hundred miles out. Already stayed late in the season for these waters."

"More than likely," Mike said. "I'm glad we made the trip out here. I always wanted to dive Guadalupe Island. Never seen so many big sea bass, anywhere. Also, some damn big lobster poking their heads out of every crevice around Adventro rock."

Joel said, "Don't forget about all the big sheepshead in that big cove. Pomene Cove, wasn't it? Gone run outta freezer space if we stay around here any longer."

"Let's get the phone calls to the L.A. office out of the way, Joel. You know how they hate calls after working hours."

The bright morning sun forced Mike to turn his head back to the long straight wake of *Blue Dolphin*. A school of porpoise playing in the wake caught his eye. He admired the activity. Something else grabbed his attention. He picked up field glasses for a better look. A sealion. *Whoa! Wait a minute. Looks like a body hung up on kelp.* He turned off the auto pilot, pulled back on the throttles. "Joel! Get your butt up here."

Joel brought in a tray from the galley, with bear claws and a decanter of hot coffee. "What's up"

"Take the helm! Looks like a body hung up on the kelp, off to port, toward the island." He pointed. "Ease us close for a better look. I'm going down. Take it slow.

Get the swim platform near as possible without disturbing anything."

"Yell out if you need me," Joel said. "The hailer will pick up your voice."

Close up, Mike saw a body. A woman. *She's alive.* He yelled, "Joel, give me a hand. Hurry, Joel."

She held out her hands. Wrists bound. she fought to keep her face above water.

Mike dove in, got his arm around her neck, face up. He kicked his way to the boat, pushed her up onto the swim platform.

Chapter 5

We need to warm her up quickly. She's nearing hypothermia. He pulled the nude woman tight against his bare torso to share his body heat.

Her shivering body spasmed violently. "Stay with me," he said. He rubbed her back vigorously. "Open your eyes and look at me."

He picked up the slim figure and climbed the three short steps from the cockpit to the lazarette deck. He glanced down at the woman's bruised face. She had one eye swollen shut, the other peeked through long dark hair.

"Joel! Rush down below and bring up a couple of thermal throws from the salon and nuke the rest of our morning coffee." *Can this be the same slim woman from the Cabo debacle? Didn't get a look at that girl's face. Yes! The same dark hair... full lips.*

Joel wrapped the girl's feet and legs. He tucked the blanket in between her naked body and Mike. He grabbed Mike's elbow and guided him through the salon to a soft L-shaped couch. Mike continued to hold the shivering woman while massaging her back.

"Bring the hot coffee, Joel. Add sugar and cream, it'll go down easier."

She tried to say something, attempted to raise her head. She stared at Mike's whiskered face. She struggled to speak again.

Mike felt her rapid heart-beat and short breaths. He spoke to her again, this time quite loud. "Look, hon, you have to take long, slow breaths. Concentrate on that. Then we'll give you a little warm coffee."

She attempted to talk again, failed. Her eyes would not leave Mike's face.

He looked down at the troubled face again, startled. *"Oh no, no, no! This can't be real.* Tracy, is it you? Tracy, please! Nod your head!" He brushed her hair away for a better look.

She moved her head up and down. Tears eased out from the inside corner of a gorgeous green eye. Mike pulled her close again. He rocked back and forth. His own tears wet sun darkened cheeks. He raised his head, in a low voice. "Thank you, God. I will never doubt you again."

Joel held a decanter of coffee with several coffee mugs on a wooden tray. He stood staring down at the confusing scene. He placed the tray on the nearby table. "What in the hell is happening, Mike? I've never seen anything like it. Tell me, so I can help."

Mike looked up at Joel. "You won't believe it, Joel. I'll fill you in after we get moving. Get us underway and on course first, at a reasonable pace. Set the auto pilot and come back, so I can tell you our story. I'm sure now. She's going to make it."

Tracy's breathing smoothed out. She reached up, attempted to put her arm around Mike's thick neck. She snuggled into his chest, shed more tears as convulsive reflexes racked her slim body. She tried again to get a few words out, to be understood. "My sister... Don't call authorities... Kill her."

Mike soon understood the few words from Tracy. "Don't call authorities, it'd mean death for her sister." He made an effort to pour coffee. Tracy held him tight, not ready to move out of the security of his arms.

Joel poured two steaming cups of coffee. He handed one to Mike. "Talk to me, Mike. I need to know what's going on. We're still on our set course of 155 degrees, making only about eight knots. I think we need to know what's happening before we rush out ahead."

Mike reached out for the coffee. "You won't believe the miracle. This battered little refugee you're looking at has been one of the most important people in my life." He tried to coax some warm coffee between Tracy's lips. "We met and fell in love many years ago, only to let life get in the way. So many lonely nights. I prayed for God to bring her back into my life. I'm convinced this horrific situation is no less than a miracle. I can't lose her now, Joel. We have some serious problems to face before this blessing's understood."

Joel poured a second cup for Mike. "We didn't know, Mike."

"We have to find out what happened to her sister. Unfortunately for Tracy, Joel, we were unaware of just what was going on back in Cabo San Lucas when we tucked tail and sailed into the sunset. We were provided with a second opportunity to save her life. Her sister's fate is still an unknown. We can't possibly leave this area without knowing what can be done for Stephanie."

Chapter 6

Mike checked the girl's pulse. Her heartbeat was strong and regular, perhaps a little fast. She'd warmed up and fallen asleep immediately.

Fascinated, he took his eyes off the sleeping girl long enough to gulp down his coffee. He was cramped up from holding her against him in an awkward position.

He gently felt around her damp scalp, looking for damage. She began to move around some, more coherent and responsive to his prompting. He lifted her bruised face, kissed the sunburned nose tenderly, speaking in a soft voice. "Please, honey, we have to get as many facts as you can give us before we make an attempt to locate your sister. Sit up and talk to me. I can make you more comfortable and let you get some rest after we have all you can tell us about her captors. Are you warming up? Nod your head."

Tracy nodded her head. She made an effort to pull the warm blanket over full breasts pressed against Mike's bare chest. She opened one eye and looked at him from a battered face. She tried to smile.

Mike pulled the blanket in between them, and eased her over to the side, into a more comfortable position on the corner of the couch where he'd been sitting.

Joel poured a second cup of coffee for Tracy. "What do we do, Mike?" He received no answer and returned to the helm.

Mike eased the cup to her lips with his hand in back of her matted hair. "We have to have information, honey. So, we can decide what to do about your sister."

She strained to look at him, one eye swollen shut. "Thank you. I have to get this out in case something else happens. It was all about drugs. It must be a big operation." She looked around. "Please, Mike. I need something to wear. Would you have something warm I could put on? I'm very uncomfortable without clothing. I'm also embarrassed. You and your friend have done all you can without making me feel ashamed."

Mike headed toward the stairs. He turned and smiled. "I've just what you need. He returned moments later with his arms full. I have two sisters who spend a great deal of time aboard. You'll be able to find what you need once you're strong enough to move about. I couldn't resist the sweats though."

Tracy attempted to smile. She reached for a well-worn workout suit. In spite of her effort to remain calm, tears trickled down her bruised cheek. "You remembered our time in sweats. I'm very unsteady, Mike. Can you help me to someplace I can get dressed?"

Mike lifted her to her feet. She staggered on weak legs, hugging the blanket. He helped her down below into the master state room. "Look through those lockers and drawers. Feel free to use anything in here. After you're dressed, maybe you can answer a few questions. It's imperative we do what we can for your sister if it isn't too late."

"Yes. Please stay with me. I just need a moment of privacy." She turned, tossed the blanket on the bed, and walked into the dressing room.

Mike watched Tracy walk away from him. His eyes followed the long, attractive legs and body. *She's taken good care of herself, physically. I hope the rest of her life has been as well cared for. What else is new? Husband? Family? Children? All in due time I suppose.*

Tracy dressed hurriedly and returned to Mike. She looked much better. He led her up to the salon deck, then into the glass enclosed pilot house.

Joel nodded, his concentration captured by a few images of distant objects on a large radar screen.

Mike followed her with his eyes. He was reminded again of that classic beauty and personal bearing that never seemed obvious to the girl.

The upper station was designed for additional crew, a soft leather couch sat on a raised platform behind two identical high captain's chairs. Its length reached the port bulkhead where a teak table was mounted beneath the large port side window and navigator's station. A full decanter of coffee and plate with pastries looked inviting to Mike. *Joel's very thoughtful this morning.*

Joel stepped away from the helm to pour two cups of coffee. He placed one on a tray near Tracy with a cream-filled donut within easy reach before speaking. "Where's that waterlogged little thing we plucked out of the Pacific Ocean?"

She attempted to smile. "Thanks, with all my heart, Joel. I remember you offering help to my sister and me in Cabo. Thanks again for that."

Mike answered for Joel. "I hate to rush this, guys. I have a strong feeling that time may be running out for Tracy's sister. We need to figure out what's going on as soon as possible."

Tracy began telling her story. "My younger sister, Stephanie, a middle school teacher in Santa Barbara, met this guy Lance Howell, at a beach volleyball tournament. She let herself get involved way too soon. I'll wait to fill in most details. She accepted an invitation for sun and sea that turned into a nightmare. She was frightened and asked if I could fly to Cabo San Lucas at once. Her purse, with all personal possessions, had disappeared soon after meeting Lance at his boat. He kept promising to take care of everything. Frustration and suspicion led her to reach out for my help. I was the logical one to ask."

Tracy sipped at her coffee, taking a long breath. "I flew down at once and met Steffi and Lance at the small boat harbor where she directed me. Lance had a nice, expensive looking yacht. I felt everything was going to work out. Stef and I finally began to relax on the aft deck, enjoying the beautiful weather. We tried to arrive at some logical answer to the problem."

She stopped to clear her thoughts. "Lance returned and apologized for having to meet with business associates in the afternoon. He soon left again with the visitors only to return later asking us to join him for dinner. He said everything would be all right. A man would meet us at the restaurant with Stephanie's hand bag. Later, ready for dinner, I realized that my own purse with my return airline ticket and personal possessions had also disappeared. I panicked briefly. Lance said he had friends joining us with everything. It had been taken by one of the men who visited Lance earlier. The man had taken the bags but would return them to us at the restaurant. We felt more or less at his mercy and agreed to stay through dinner. Lance drove us to the restaurant in a nice SUV. Everything started to become more and more contentious there, as we questioned him and didn't like the answers we were getting. I suggested to Steffi that we leave and call a taxi. I only had a few dollars in my pocket. You know pretty much what happened afterwards at the restaurant."

She asked Joel for a glass of water. "As soon as Hondo and Turk Guerrero appeared at our table, I knew we were in trouble. We stood up to leave when Lance demanded we sit down and stay put. I stood again and slapped him hard across his face. He became furious, and hit me back, very hard. We were told he'd make the decisions for both of us."

Her voice grew hoarser. "We had no choice. Hondo and Turk dragged us outside and tied us in a rear seat of some old van. We were taken to a dirty warehouse, stayed there until after dark, then taken to Lance's boat. We were locked in a small cabin with two beds and a toilet. That's where we remained. Turk brought in rice and beans with two water bottles twice a day."

She reached for more water. "Some time the second day we heard the motors start up. Several people were talking loudly. From there I sort of lost track of what was going on. We went fast all day and night. The air in our cabin was stale and the boat was pounding hard against the waves. We were both sick the whole time. We tried to sleep. Then, the next day, one of the men came down and told us he would release us with the full freedom of the boat if we'd cooperate and cause no trouble. We were given crew duties and allowed to move about the boat. I heard them use the radio a lot. They had some sort of special telephone for talking to Lance. I could hear them talking to each other from the salon. They often talked to other ships or boats. It became obvious that drugs and people were being moved around on boats they called pangas. They were afraid of Lance but couldn't understand why they couldn't have fun with Steff and me."

She stopped for a moment. "On the second or third day at sea, they locked us in our cabin and told us to be quiet or they wouldn't be responsible for what might happen to us. We could hear a lot of loud talking in Spanish and talking on the phone. That went on all day. We heard other boat motors start up and fairly soon our boat started up. We were later released and told to prepare food and coffee. I felt like we cruised all night. About four a.m., Turk came down to the galley for coffee. I heard Hondo above on the phone. It was clear he was talking to Lance. It became obvious things were changing."

Tracy choked-up, wiping tears away. "Turk went below to the aft deck and brought up a small anchor and some chain. I thought we might be going to anchor near an island I'd seen two or three times over the last few days. Then I heard Hondo tell Turk to go ahead with the dark-haired woman. I panicked. I woke Steffi. Turk came into our cabin. He tied Stephanie's hands together. We started screaming and fighting. He called out to Hondo for help and they locked Stefany in the cabin while Turk went back to the boat controls."

Tracy reached for another tissue. "Hondo dragged me into the salon, violently stripped all my clothing off, including my underwear. I scratched his face and bit him hard on his shoulder before he tied my hands together. Turk started screaming for Hondo, telling him to come to the radio. That's when I broke away and ran out on deck."

She looked at Mike. "I was sure they were going to rape me and tie the anchor around my body before shoving me overboard. I heard Steffi screaming and slamming herself against the door. I looked up and saw the silhouette of the island in the moonlight. It looked so close-by. I'm a very good swimmer. I felt like taking this last gamble was much better than the alternative. The island seemed near, yet so far."

She pulled away from Mike's shoulder. "I jumped, turned on my back and kicked with my legs. Some of the time I would stop to rest on my back with just my face out of the water. The sound of the boat faded away in the dark. The sky started getting brighter and I knew I was getting weaker. I was so afraid they would turn around and come back for me. I soon realized my body temperature was dropping. That's when I spotted a thick patch of kelp. I thought it would keep me afloat while I rested. I didn't hear your boat until just before I turned and saw a huge unshaven man looking down at me. I must have been there a long time."

Mike and Joel stared at Tracy, fascinated.

Mike reached out and wrapped her in his arms again. He held her, ever so gently, his eyes clouding up. *So many questions to ask.*

"Tracy, we have to act on this problem right away. You've been through a lot. Still, we need to think about what can be done to locate Stephanie. To do nothing is not an option. She could become a victim of abuse before we get there. Time is of the essence.

He looked at his dive watch. "You can relax a while and get rested up. We're going to need you on the planning session. I suggest you go through the clothes in my sister's state room until you find what you need. Take a hot shower with a short rest. Those quarters are yours for the duration of the trip, so get yourself comfortable in there."

Shit! I forgot. He'd blanked on it. "Oh, before you go, would you care to call your family?"

"No! I can't face that until I know what's happened to Stephanie." She threw her hand out. "Wait, Mike! I remember hearing them say they're going to stay in the vicinity of Guadalupe Island and refuel from some kind of large ship. That had to be important."

"Thanks, Tracy. That's very important. Go on down. We have it for now."

Mike and Joel sat a few minutes before Joel spoke up. "We're only about eight nautical miles from Guadalupe Island. I think we'd better return and stick close by until we get a handle on this thing."

"That's my thinking precisely, Joel. Set a reciprocal course taking us back to the island at about ten knots? We can lay in close to the northeast quarter of the island, put out a dive flag and lower the small tender. We should drop the hook as close to shore as possible. That way, we give the appearance of continuing the dive pattern already established. We'll ride out the rest of the daylight on anchor."

Mike looked away from the chart. "After dark, we cruise down the leeward side of the island using the radar. Got to stay well away from any cluster of vessels. Use the long-range radar to pick out targets we think might be that big sports fisher. Then we break out the high intensity night vision binoculars for a closer look."

Joel listened carefully, then spoke up. "You know I'm in agreement one hundred percent on this caper, Mike. But it's my duty to point out that you have a hell of a lot to lose here. I don't want to be the bearer of bad news if things go really bad."

"That said, Joel. Let's make things happen. We're still in Mexican waters. As insurance, we break out the hidden cache of emergency weapons"

"For sure, they're of no use to us hidden below decks, Mike."

"We already know how vicious our adversaries are, Joel. We'd better be dedicated to success at all cost. It's self-defense first. The Mexican authorities aren't going to be helpful with this situation, only harmful to us, maybe more so than the narco crowd. They're connected at the hip."

Tracy followed Mike's instructions and went below into the most fabulous quarters she'd ever seen on a boat. Soft polished teakwood décor blended with the amazing quality of other furnishings. She kneeled near the big soft bed, placed elbows down, hands cupped beneath her chin. *Thank you, Lord, for the miracles of today,*

Lord, my life being a part of today's blessings. I'm sure you understand what I mean, Lord. This big unshaven person has returned into my life at a most unexpected and critical period of need. He may now have a family of his own, dear Lord, and if he does, I promise there'll be no interference on my part. I sense that he still has that once strong affection and passion that was evident so many years ago. Should such blessing be freely offered without encumbrances to this humble person, I'll accept with gratitude. Most important, Lord, bestow your blessings upon my sister, Stephanie, so that she may be released from the vicious persons who hold her prisoner. Save her life, Lord, please. Our Father in Heaven.

After a shower and a brief rest, she returned to the pilot house dressed in neat, clean blue jeans, a clean white tee shirt and white boating shoes.

"Mike. I'm indebted to someone with exquisite taste for these comfortable clothes. I'll do my best to take care of them."

"My sisters would be pleased to have you share with them."

"Have I missed anything, guys? I'm afraid you'll have to continue looking at this ugly puss a while longer. I tried makeup, then removed it, after realizing it only made me look more ridiculous."

Mike and Tracy stood alone in the well-equipped ship's galley. Tracy looked at everything. She opened one cabinet after the other, reviewed the refrigerated foods, frozen foods and pastry selections, each in their own protective case. Mike reached across, in front of Tracy, his arm touching the sensitive tip of a breast. Both reacted. Acutely aware of each other. Their eyes met. Mike pulled Tracy to his chest. He held her there. "I don't want to make you uncomfortable, Tracy. But I'm so pleased to have you here. Are you going to leave again?"

"I think I understand, Mike. We don't really know each other any more. We were frank and open with each other in that more innocent life, so young. I feel that I knew you well and trust in your integrity and good judgment. I see you have many of the same questions I have. Hold me for a few moments, please. Then let's help Steffi. I promise to be open and receptive to discuss our personal dilemma once we've helped my sister.

He released her and she shifted her attention back to the chores at hand. "Mike, is it okay if I take over the galley duties? I want to help, not just take up space. I'll still be available to assist anywhere else as well. You go on up. I'll make lunch."

Tracy served a lunch of thick roast beef sandwiches, potato chips and cold beer. Afterwards, they relaxed on the sun deck.

Blue Dolphin swung on anchor in the calm water near Guadalupe Island, waiting for dark. Mike and Joel stretched out in the sun with only fishing shorts for protection from the tropical sun. Both men teased Tracy, asking her to don one of the several bikinis available.

Minutes later, she surprised them when she returned topside in a small blue bikini, nearly matching her tan lines. Her full breasts overwhelmed the tiny bra top. Both Mike and Joel quickly offered to apply the necessary sunscreen.

Tracy laughed out loud in her well-remembered deep voice.

Mike thought, *Thank God she still has her spirit.*

She said, "Not today, guys," and slipped on sunglasses and a wide brim hat. "You two need to concentrate on our rescue plan." She sat down in a reclining deck chair between the two men with a wide smile across her face.

Chapter 7

Mike paced the deck, deep in thought. His analysis of the facts painted a dark picture for the girl held captive. *Any action is better than no action,* he thought. His give-no-quarter nature.

He settled in next to Tracy. "I've been thinking this thing through. It's bigger than we could have imagined. We can't leave here without finding Stephanie, at least find that boat, her last known location. From this point on, we need to be alert for that sport fisher, and any other vessel that looks suspicious. We'll remain here on anchor until we figure things out."

He put down his beer, ran fingers through thick sun-bleached hair. "We're blessed with very calm conditions here on the lee side of the island. Joel and I need some rest to stay sharp for tonight's work. Here's what we do."

Mike took off his cap to wipe sweat off his brow. "Starting now, Joel. You take the first watch from the upper control station for about an hour. Tracy, you go down and get some rest, then take the second watch here on the bridge for an hour. Just report any boating activity at all to me. I'll take the third watch. By that time, we'll give the impression of visiting sport divers resting up at cocktail time. We'll hang here on anchor flying the dive flag, keeping a sharp eye out for that boat."

He turned down the volume on the emergency channel and sat down again. "Now, listen. Here's how things stand. We're in Mexican waters and that means no help from the authorities. We'll be acting just as much outside the law as the narco guys. We know they're vicious killers. They'll kill us all given the chance. Our only hope of success is stealth. Once they become aware of us as adversaries, our advantage is gone. We must agree on a plan, act fast, be quiet, and deadly aggressive. We're assuming the narco vessel remains in nearby waters, somewhere around Guadalupe Island. If that assumption is correct, we have a slim chance of success."

He looked at Tracy and Joel. "Anything to add so far?"

She shook her head.

Mike continued. "Stephanie's only chance depends on our locating her whereabouts and taking aggressive action before the brothers do. If we stir up the hornets' nest too soon, without acting, there's very little chance of survival. Their vessel is likely nearby. They're not going to be cruising around burning up critical fuel. I think they'll be lying on anchor in an isolated bight somewhere on the lee side of Guadalupe Island."

Mike removed his long bib cap, massaged his temple firmly and finished off his beer before continuing. "Joel, I'd like for you to go below into the lazarette shop after your watch and prepare two separate sections of anchor chain. Each about three feet long. Do you think we can scrape up a couple of padlocks?"

"I believe so, Mike. I'm sure we can confiscate a couple off those chests holding extra dive gear."

"That's good. While you're taking care of that, I'll lay out everything we need for cocktails and dinner in the upper salon." He looked at Tracy. "How would you like a big meal of grilled seabass, grilled asparagus spears and twice baked potatoes? All left by the family. After that we pick up the discussion and plan the evening's work."

Tracy said, "That sounds delicious Mike, I'll help with that."

Joel looked concerned. "So, you plan on immobilizing that big vessel by wrapping a chain around each of the two props and locking them to the strut. That should do the job all right. Now the difficult part! How do we get that damn heavy load to the vessel without being detected?"

"That's the tough part. We must locate the vessel. Then we give those on-board time to go down for the night, hoping they're confident enough to feel secure without an anchor watch. Tracy, have you handled a tender or small boat before?"

"I've driven outboards, and a friend's inboard on waterskiing outings at Lake Mead. I can handle it, Mike."

"Okay. Once we've located and scouted the target, we'll use the smaller tender. We can attach the small electric trolling motor onto the transom next to the outboard. We have scuba equipment and night vision gear onboard. If no one's on watch during the two to 3:00 three a.m. period, we may not need the scuba gear. If we spot a night watch onboard, then we have Tracy lay off a reasonable distance and wait, while we go in under water."

Mike took several deep swallows from the water bottle. "We wrap each short section of chain around a flotation device. Four feet of light weight chain, like that used for the tenders or the stern anchors, won't sink a life vest. But when wrapped, it should compress the vest down to a smaller silhouette. Then we tow the bundle using thirty or forty feet of parachute cord from our shark fishing gear, secured with a snap fastener. If our luck holds and no watch is posted, we motor close enough to use the electric motor for Tracy to drop us in the shadow of the sport fisher. That way Joel and I can push our load underneath the swim step. Once on board in bare feet and swim trunks, our best weapon will be the dive knife strapped to our leg."

He stopped for a moment. "Tracy! Remember not to let the tender bump against the side of our target. A small sound on the outside is magnified on the inside and will wake the occupants. Now, tell us about the layout of this boat we have to board."

She nodded. "All the cabins are up front. A large room in front with two smaller rooms across from each other down the narrow hallway leading from the salon to the forward cabin. If you enter from the swim step, go through the cockpit, straight on through the salon and galley, then down to the room on the right, where Stefanie should be. The men use the room on the left. There's a spiral stair-case in the salon that leads to the flying bridge where the controls and radios are located. The upper bridge area is a large and comfortable room with a long seat in front of the helm."

She hesitated a moment. "I have a feeling that one of the men may be sleeping on that wide padded bench seat. I often took food and coffee up to the men. One of them was always stretched out on that seat and leaning against the window. I'm worried about Stefanie, guys. If you attempt to enter her room, she may scream and kick, waking up the other men. What should we do?"

"I know. That occurred to me as well. Ideas, Joel?"

"Yeah, here's the thing. We can't allow the guy on the bridge to get to the radio. A call out would insure our destruction. So, we must secure the bridge first."

"That means, at all costs, Joel. We can't be lucky enough to trap both men in the cabins below."

Mike hesitated a few moments. "We should be moving soon if we hope to locate that boat. We'll set a course for the more protected south end of the island using the long-range radar to stay well away from the shoreline. We investigate each of the targets showing a favorable radar signature."

He nudged Tracy. "This is going to be a long night. Why don't you bring up the single-cup coffee maker and assorted midnight rations to keep us going through the night? When you get back, we'll continue our skull session. Meanwhile, I'll get the tenders ready with everything we need for the operation."

Mike and Joel continued talking quietly until Tracy returned from her third trip below with enough K-Cups, pastries and wrapped sandwiches for twice as many people.

Mike nudged Joel. "It's time to move. Pull the stern anchor and prepare to get underway as planned."

Mike passed a cup of coffee to Tracy. "Once we step onto the swim platform. I want you to back off a safe distance and wait. We've agreed that I'll secure the bridge. Joel's going to stand by in the passageway between the two cabins. If, and when, I get the bridge secured without too much noise, Joel will hold his position. I'll let you know when to come around to the swim step where I'll tie off the tender."

Moonlight reflected off the water, lighting up the nearby island. Joel said. "Moving in closer was a good idea. We've cruised for two hours and the best prospect was about five miles back, that large white boat glaring in the bright moonlight."

Mike said, "Cruise around the south end at a leisurely pace of six knots, Joel. Take us past the suspect boat. None of the other radar silhouettes are large enough and they don't fit the profile. Make the return at roughly fifty yards from shore. We can get a good picture of everything on the way back without attracting attention. I think it wise to make a midnight surveillance run first with the larger tender."

"Okay, Mike. Have Tracy flip a coin to see which of us takes the first run. We both can't go."

Fishing for a coin, Mike said, "Here, Tracy. My lucky quarter. I take heads."

Joel said, "I don't trust either of you. Go ahead and flip it."

Tracy called out, "Heads," then said, "Oh shit, Mike. let me go with you. Please." She looked at him, ready to beg if necessary.

Joel said, "I told you so."

After a moment of thought Mike looked at Tracy's face. "Okay. You're a big part of this operation from beginning to end.

"Joel, it's nearly one a.m. I think I recall a small headland about a mile past what looks like our target. That should shield *Blue Dolphin* from a radar silhouette. Put out at least an eight to one scope to hold us in place. Use the heavier starboard anchor. I'm going out on the boat deck and switch the electric motor over to the larger tender. Just in case of trouble, I want a nine-millimeter under the helm of each tender before we launch. Let's hope we don't need to use them."

He caught Tracy's eye. "Go down and find yourself a dark, pullover, long-sleeved shirt. Don't want it too heavy in case we take to the water, but it'll get cold on the tender, speeding across the water this time of night."

Joel said, "The anchor is well set, launch the RIB Mike. So you know, we're anchored just at the outer tip of the headland. Our radar silhouette will blend with the island and allow me to watch you on radar. Just don't get caught. You can use the tender radio if necessary. It's set on channel twelve. I'll monitor it, with plenty of others. You guys be careful and come back home to papa with all the right answers."

The four-stroke outboard started at once. Mike engaged the drive gear and moved away. He turned to Tracy. "Move to the rear and locate the electric control switch on the small electric motor next to the big motor." He'd explained the use prior to launching. "Go ahead, Tracy. You have control. I'll kill the big engine."

Tracy moved the control to a slow setting and maneuvered the craft from side to side, increasing speed. "It's so quiet. I only hear movement of water,"

"Okay, any more questions?"

"No. I'm starting the bigger motor, then turning it off."

"Okay, kid. Get over here beneath the wheel."

Tracy grabbed the wheel, reached for the ignition key, turned the key to start. Nothing happened. She looked at Mike.

"Move the shifter to neutral. The starter won't engage unless it's in neutral."

"Got-cha." Tracy moved the shifter back and forth a few times, found the neutral position. The engine started. She engaged the gear, moved off. After a few sharp, back and forth turns, she turned control over to Mike. He and Tracy headed south, hugging the coastline.

Mike said, "Stop! A large boat appeared near the shoreline, outlined against the night sky. "That's it. There can't be more than one big, customized sports fisher like that within a thousand miles." He passed the light-sensitive binoculars to Tracy. "Tell me what you think."

"That does look like the boat. I remember those two big tanks on top of that arch thing with all those antennas."

Mike explained, "You're looking at satellite navigation and telephone equipment. Hold us here near the shore. I need to study this thing with the night vision equipment."

After fifteen or twenty minutes of careful observation, Mike removed the night vision headset and placed the harness over Tracy's head. "Move this little lever up and down for focus."

Tracy adjusted the lever back and forth a little. "This is fantastic. It's eerie with that bright yellow glow all over things. I can see it all much better. It's almost like looking outside just before dawn breaks."

"Okay, hurry now. Let me have the headset. It's time to go before someone pops up to take-a-look around. The current's carrying us in their direction."

Chapter 8

"We have no choice here. *Blue Dolphin* must be left on anchor with no one onboard," Mike said. "Tracy, are you sure about your part in this scheme?"

They crowded into the small tender. "Yes, Mike! My safety's not an issue, you know that."

"Okay then. If our luck holds, we'll get Steffi into the tender with you immediately. Remember to lay off away from the boat about fifty feet to wait for Joel and me. If you hear gunfire, move even farther away and wait for us to call you by name. You'll know it's time to use the gun under the helm, if the brothers show up outside without us. Joel, can you think of anything else before we shove off?"

"No, the *Dolphin* is well hooked. Let's see what we can do about those guys holding Stephanie."

With Tracy at the controls, they approached with caution, within a hundred feet of the large vessel. A breeze rippled the water and a soft slapping sound came from the larger vessel.

Mike saw no one on watch. He whispered, "Hold it right here. No sign of a night watch. Once we're out, move into the shadows near shore until we signal you to come in close."

Mike and Joel wore fishing shorts, T-shirt, fins and dive masks, prepared for a swim.

"Don't need the cord, Joel. Let the flotation devices float away after we reach our target. There'll be some rattling of the chain. Work slow, it'll be mistaken for anchor chain dragging over the rocky bottom. You secure the port propeller first, while I watch for any activity onboard. Once the port side propeller is secured, climb into the cockpit with your knife ready while I secure the starboard propeller."

Both propellers were locked tight with a minimum amount of noise. Mike eased onto the swim step, kicked off his fins, and stepped into the cockpit. Joel slipped down into the lower passageway where sleeping quarters were located. Mike watched in the dim light as Joel wedged the blade of his heavy dive knife into the wall behind the sliding door of the small stateroom on the left, securing it temporarily.

Mike climbed the spiral ladder to the enclosed flying bridge. He saw no one, then heard a groan. A large man straightened up on the padded bench seat, rubbing his eyes. Mike moved fast. He reached for the man's hands to wrap them with duct tape. The man shouted and slammed both feet into Mike's midsection. The blow forced him back near the stairs. He recovered, faced his attacker, deflected a blow, and landed a hard right to the face. The man tumbled backwards, down the steel ladder and bounced out onto the deck below. Mike dropped down to bind both hands with duct tape.

The second man cursed in Spanish and attempted to break down the door. Joel had all his weight pressed against the strong knife jammed into the wall, preventing the sliding door from opening. He shouted at Mike, "What do we do now?"

"On my signal, retrieve your knife and step back to your right. That'll put his momentum toward me. Watch for a weapon of some kind."

The door flew open, propelling the man toward Mike. He slashed out wildly with a long blade. Mike delivered a lightning blow to the man's face. His fist landed underneath the chin, into the exposed throat, crushing the larynx. The man dropped to his knees gasping for breath.

Joel kicked the knife away, then reached down to bind the man's hands.

Mike touched his shoulder. "Don't bother. I don't think he'll make it. His throat's swelling rapidly. Keep an eye on him."

Joel stared back at Mike. "Look at your hip! Are you okay to keep going?"

Mike looked down at a long cut across his right hip just below the beltline, a ten-inch gash. His fishing shorts were sliced open, barely staying up. He saw the cut was shallow yet, bleeding profusely. "Yeah, I felt something. Check to be sure we're alone first. Then wave in the tender. Tie it to the transom. Ask Tracy to come aboard while I find the key for the locked room." He listened at the door, feeling better at once. He'd detected a tearful, feminine cough.

Mike turned his full attention back to the assailant on the deck. The man struggled for one last breath before falling on his side. Mike noticed a ring of keys clipped to the man's belt. He bent down, felt for a carotid artery, detected no pulse, then released the snap ring holding keys to the belt.

Joel, checked the master's suite quickly, moved on to check the other assailant at the bottom of the stairs, taped earlier by Mike. He detected no pulse or breathing.

Joel said, "We're all alone here Mike." He walked outside and waved Tracy over.

He tied off the tender quickly, signaling her to remain seated. "Everything's good. We believe Stephanie's in her cabin where you thought she'd be. Mike's been injured. He isn't letting on about it but he may be losing too much blood. Go in and help him free your sister while I look for a first aid kit. All vessels of this size have something to serve that purpose. His wound is shallow. Perhaps we can pull it closed with tape."

Mike waved Tracy inside, switching on lights in the narrow hallway. He quickly found the key to the room Stefanie was believed to be in. He analyzed the situation at hand and decided on a course of action in light of what just happened, two dead bodies.

Tracy attempted to ignore the man curled up on the floor. She stared at the open gash across Mike's hip. Blood ran down his leg and off his bare foot. "The bleeding appears to have slowed or stopped. Are you all right?" She bent down for a better look at the wide-open wound. The dim light in the passageway made the scene appear bad.

"I'm okay. We have to release Stephanie and see if she's injured. Are you ready?"

"What do we do?"

"Stand back until we're sure there's no surprise waiting for us inside there with Stefanie."

Mike unlocked the door and eased it back for a look into the dark room. He saw a small frame curled up with a pillow making a quiet sniffling sound. He stepped aside and gestured for Tracy to go in. He pointed at the figure on one of the beds.

Tracy whispered, "Stef, it's me." She placed a hand on a shoulder.

Stephanie raised her head quickly, grabbing at her sister.

Tracy let herself fall onto the bed. "Oh God, oh God, oh God." Both women sobbed together quietly.

Mike said, "Look girls, it's late and we still have work to do. Come on outside." He hurried past the body in the salon, on into the cockpit. "Are you okay, Stephanie?"

She tipped her head up, smiling. "Thank you both so much. I don't know who you are, but it must be a miracle. I thought for sure Tracy was gone. Hondo and Turk said she jumped overboard with her hands tied."

Mike nudged the girls toward the tender. "We can catch up with everything after we're back onboard *Blue Dolphin.* Hurry now. We'll lose the darkness soon. Joel! Take the girls to the boat and hurry back. We have to search this thing and prepare it for our final departure."

He watched them move away then checked on the man he'd knocked down the staircase into the salon. As suspected, a broken neck. He'd never regained consciousness. Two dead people. *It's just as well. We have nothing to lose now by covering our tracks.*

He moved on to the main salon and searched it well. So far, he'd located two separate hideaways. The first was in the center of the king size bed, beneath the mattress, a light gauge metal box with locked lid mounted securely to the wooden frame and covered over with a simple thin throw rug. None of the keys from the ring fit the lock. He thought it would be simple to breach with the right tool. The second hideaway was a large open space behind a full-size hinged mirror on the starboard bulkhead. He found three short rows of ladies' handbags on shelves. He felt sure the girls would be able to identify their own among the many. Next, he checked the large shower and toilet facility, including a small dressing table and mirror inside the enclosure. He found nothing unusual there. He entered the larger room where the two brothers kept their belongings while on board. There he found two personal wallets for the brothers with their identifications and a small amount of cash. He opened one of two hanging lockers, picked up a dark blue canvas bag filled with US currency. He thumbed through tightly packed bundles of cash, mostly fifty- or hundred-dollar bills.

Joel returned to see Mike sitting there looking at the open bag. "You found the money tree, huh?"

Mike nodded. "This stash has to be the brothers' expense money or money to pay associates."

"Mike, your wound. You can't neglect that thing. Let's take a minute to clean it up properly. Otherwise, it might get infected. Bleeding seems to have stopped."

Joel poured peroxide into a gauze pad and cleaned the wound. He found what he needed in a medical kit on the bridge. He pulled the long cut closed and taped it tight. Then he applied a temporary bandage over the entire thing.

Mike stood and moved about. "Joel. I hope you agree with me. I've given a lot of thought to this thing. Our best option is to do away with any sign of our presence here. We need to scuttle this boat, sending the whole thing down where the water's deep enough to hide what happened from the cartel. She's hooked on the edge of an underwater cliff now. We can let out another few hundred feet of chain on this beauty and use the tender to tow her off to the east where the depth drops off fast. With the props locked up like they are, it may be a simple matter of revving those large engines and slamming it in gear. Something will give way.

Either the struts will rip loose or the engines will break loose from the engine mounts, ripping loose the saltwater intake."

Joel said, "To begin with, let me find something to pry open that metal locker in the bed." Within minutes, he returned from the tool locker with a medium size pry bar. "This should do the job." It took only minutes to open the box, finding it filled with more hard cash. The locker was deeper than expected. "We can't leave this filthy stuff in here to pollute the water, can we?"

Mike reached in the closet for another canvas bag. It was full of clothes. He emptied out the bag before handing it to Joel who began filling it with the cash. "One should be enough don't you think? We need to hurry and get loaded up, get this trunk on the bottom before daylight, if possible."

Loading everything into the tender, Joel said, "Let's slash the intake hoses first, to be sure she fills with water. Then we'll open deck hatches in the cockpit and cutoff electricity to the bilge pumps. Flip to see who starts up the engines." He flipped the coin, grinning. "You lose, big guy. I get the honors. I'll join you in a jiffy."

They moved through the boat rapidly. "She's ready for the dive, Mike. I tied a tow line to the tender, move her on out while I fire up the engines on this baby."

He started the engines and engaged both transmissions. Moments later he opened the throttle on both big diesels and raced to the railing. He looked around first, then slipped under the railing into the tender with Mike.

Mike gunned the throttle. The ninety horsepower outboard had no problem swinging the stern of the big boat out toward deeper water. "Listen to that!" he said. A loud screaming noise came from the stressed transmissions. Another ripping, banging noise also filled the air when one and then the other rear struts securing the propeller shaft to the boat hull broke away, flinging the heavy chain around. Water rushed in to fill the rear cavity of the vessel. The open hatch above where the strut was fastened to the hull had water spraying three feet above the deck.

The anchor chain stretched tight. Mike said, "That's it. The stern quarter's dipping under. Cast off the line and let's head home."

Joel scanned the sky and horizon before commenting, "Lucky for us there've been no signs of aircraft or other boating activity in the area since yesterday afternoon. Hey, look! The engines are still racing as she goes below the surface. There must be an air pocket in the engine room."

The sky was growing lighter when Mike looked at *Blue Dolphin*. Tracy and Stefanie stood on deck waiting, then hurried down into the cockpit.

Tracy said, "Is everything okay, Mike? We were getting concerned."

"Thanks, Tracy. It all went well. I hope you both have rested some and found a bite to eat. Joel and I are bushed. Relief on Tracy's face was obvious to him. "You ladies should go ahead and get settled in for a good six to eight hours' rest. We have a lot to talk about, but it can wait. There's a long voyage ahead. We may each be assigned a standby watch while we're at sea and take turns napping."

He sat down and looked at Joel. "We'd better clear this area now, without obvious haste. The sun will be up before we clear the northern tip of the island. Check the weather first, Joel. Then put us underway on course zero degrees magnetic. We have about four hundred miles of open sea ahead. I'm concerned about a chance encounter with one of the cartel's large host vessels the Guerrero brothers were in communication with. That guy Lance may have checked us out, identified the *Dolphin*, and spread the word."

Joel nodded. "I'll take care of the tenders and get us seaworthy, then under way. You don't look too good, Mike."

He grinned. "Thanks, do that for me, please."

Mike returned to the bridge after a brief cleanup. "I'll take the first turn on watch, Joel. Before the girls turn in for some rest, help them report in with a phone call to their parents or other family. Would you mind doing that? I believe I should stay in the background until I hear more about Tracy's home life. She's being closemouthed about her personal history."

Chapter 9

"I panicked, Stephanie! That island looked close enough I could swim right to it. I swam for an hour, looked up and it seemed farther away. I realized my strength was going. I tried to rest for a moment on a kelp bed. When I opened my eyes, a huge unshaven man seemed to appear out of the sea itself. I thought it was a trick of the mind, was so tired my eyes blurred."

She wiped away a tear before continuing. "Mike has been so gracious. He never hesitated. He wanted to find you. He's unaware of my deep secret, sis. I feel so guilty not sharing with him years ago." She accepted a hand full of tissue from Stephanie.

Mike and Joel returned to *Blue Dolphin*. They looked to be well worn down.

Tracy spotted Mike's injury immediately. She pulled the bloody garment away. "Mike, you've re-injured yourself. We need to take care of this now. You're still losing blood. Let me help you."

"Give me a minute, please. I've a couple things to do first."

Joel came in with bags in both hands. "Here, Tracy, catch." He heaved a large plastic bag onto the deck at her feet.

"This is for you, Stephanie." He placed a small, neat travel case in front of her.

She squealed with delight. "That's my travel case! I thought it was gone forever. Thanks, Joel!"

Joel stored the two canvas bags in the dive compartment and returned to steady up the tenders for open sea.

Mike sat down on the raised couch behind the helm. "We have a lot to talk about and more to do."

Tracy sat down next to Mike. She patiently waited to get his attention. *Should I butt in? He needs to get that injury cleaned immediately.*

"Joel! Do you feel like handling the bridge? I need about an hour and then you can take an eight-hour rest. You won't have to be on deck again until four this afternoon."

Tracy said, "Mike. You need to do something about that injury. At least let me pull it together with tape. It should be cleaned first."

Mike nodded.

Joel said, "I can handle things here, Mike. You take the time you need. I'll keep us on our course, due north, into San Diego, right?"

"That's it, Joel. The latest weather report indicated we'd have uncommonly good weather for the next three hundred miles. After that, it'll get rough. We could have some problems with a pressure gradient predicted off Southern California."

Tracy watched Mike sag into one of the raised command chairs before continuing. She admired his stamina.

Joel said, "We'll take our time for the next thirty-six hours. It's possible we'll miss the worst of those winds."

"A good chance of that. We should have about three hundred miles of decent weather. She's in your hands, Joel. I'll see you here in about an hour."

Mike turned to Tracy, "Why don't you get Stephanie settled in your cabin then give me a hand. I'll be in D suite getting cleaned up. Each stateroom has a medical kit. Just come in when you can."

Tracy opened the plastic bag, looked inside, then dumped everything out onto the deck. "Look, Stef, here's my purse." She grabbed it, looked through it quickly and pulled out a phone, then her wallet. She checked to be sure her credit cards and identification were intact. "Wheee-ee! What a relief. What purse did you have, Steph?"

Stephanie closed her travel case, then stepped back to look at Tracy and the many handbags scattered there on the carpeted salon. "There! That one over there," she said, pointing at a large stylish bag near Tracy. Stephanie stepped around the variety of bags and picked up the one indicated. She knew at once that it was her missing handbag.

"This is my bag, Tracy. That low life bastard, had our bags all along. You suppose these other handbags belong to more missing women?"

"Stephanie, it's time you and I opened our eyes. This kind of evil is so close to us, the people we mingle with. I would never expect normal looking people like that jerk Lance to be capable of such brutality. Let's face it. You and I are fortunate to be alive and here to talk about it. The women who lost those bags, may have lost their lives."

Tracy knocked, and entered the room. Mike sat in a comfortable chair drying his blond hair with a large towel. He'd dressed in a clean white T-shirt and boxer shorts. His trim physique didn't go unnoticed by Tracy. Still unsure about things, she hesitated, then gained control. *Old feelings die hard*, she thought. "Mike, you, lovable miscreant. I can't stand much of this."

"I know, Tracy. We need to talk. I'm going crazy, not knowing everything about you and your family. You can't know how I fantasized about a miraculous reunion. Never dreamed it'd be like this."

"It's not fair for you to say such things, Mike. You must have a beautiful family of your own by now after all these years."

"Never found the right one after you. I looked at every woman I went out with, hoping to find some of you hiding inside. My father once accused me of acting like a blind dung beetle running around, looking for a hole in a concrete pasture. He may have been right, because I'm still looking for that special something or someone that I once found, only to lose way too soon."

"Are you telling me now that you've never been married? You…? A successful attractive man?"

"That's right, Tracy. I'm still hoping for that family, searching for the right partner. Now, tell me all about you, the beautiful young athletic mother-in-waiting that I remember."

"If you must know, Mike, she's still waiting for the father of her children. That's all you need to know for now. We're all tired and you don't want to keep Joel on hold. He's as tired as any of us. Let me help you dress your injured hip. You shouldn't put it off any longer. Does this kit have all we need?"

"Yes. I cleaned the gash well with soap and water but it's difficult to reach for proper care. I'll lie on my side so you can get to it more easily". A huge smile spread across his face. "You can pull my pants down without my help."

"You're still the frisky young Turk I remember. Maybe I should've stayed on that kelp bed." She grabbed his shorts and yanked them down past his shiny white ass.

Tracy returned to the bridge to rest on the couch behind Joel. She dozed off.

Joel touched Tracy's shoulder. "You looked so tired, I hated to wake you. The sleeping troll wanted an hour of rest. He's had more than two, want to do the honors?"

Somewhat refreshed, she went down to where Mike was sleeping. She stood over him thinking of the man she'd known so long ago. She recalled tracing her fingers over the manly features of his less than perfect face. She woke him with a soft kiss and returned to the bridge.

Tracy relaxed in the second command chair and watched Mike do his thing. He appeared rested and explained what he was doing. He stayed busy, double-checked their course, projected fuel usage and tracked a large radar target. She guessed it to be a car carrier or other large ship. He showed her some instruments pertaining to the ship's mechanical and electrical systems. They appeared to be performing as they should. During slack periods, he began planning a few good meals with her. She felt tired, went down to freshen up.

At two-forty-five in the afternoon, Tracy rejoined Mike on the bridge. She'd dressed in tan shorts with a white halter top that left a narrow white strip of un-tanned breast exposed. *He noticed.* She couldn't resist, stood on her toes, and placed a light kiss on the corner of his mouth.

He smiled, then looked at Tracy's green eyes. "You know you shouldn't do this to me."

She laughed with her deep throated resonance. "I'm just offering to help with the chores. By the way, Stef asked about using the washer and dryer later today."

"Yeah, that's fine. I'm sure you'll find what you need in the laundry area. What do you think about you and I preparing a nice meal to serve here in the upper salon about four? It'd be a pleasant surprise for the others."

"That's a wonderful idea, Mike. It'll also make me feel useful. Stefanie's out cold, sleeping in that air-conditioned room."

Mike picked up a yellow note pad, handed it to Tracy. "Here, look this over. Just ideas for meals. I'd like to see us all have two good meals a day. We can snack or drink beer the rest of the time. As of now, that responsibility is yours and Stef's. Okay?"

"You got it, Mike! We'll take it from here. How about using that drop leaf in the salon for the main meals? I'm going down, Mike. I need to get familiar with what's available from the galley and food storage lockers. Can I bring you anything?"

"I could use a beer, been on a coffee diet for more than six hours."

She had a sudden urge to hug him, then resisted.

An hour later Mike pointed at a tiny yellow canary that flew in to make himself at home on a rack of martini glasses in the upper salon.

She said, "Oh, look! He's waiting for happy hour."

The fascinating little guy sat on his perch, socialized with his human companions for maybe twenty-minutes, circled around inside the room and flew away.

Mike said, "I've seen these little guys arrive miles from land, visit a short while, then fly away. I wonder where they come from?"

The blue ocean remained smooth and calm throughout the day. Tracy relaxed on the open deck with binoculars in one hand, a cold Corona in the other. She'd been watching a school of porpoise at play until a clean-shaven Joel joined her.

"Hi, Joel. You look much more rested. Can I get you anything from below? It makes me feel useful and keeps my legs from getting flabby." Before he could answer, she pointed, "Look! I can't believe the huge school of porpoise. They're everywhere."

Joel said, "Have you ever watched them from the bow? You get a different look as they jump the bow wake, swim in and out, from underneath the boat."

"That sounds like fun. Is it safe out there?"

"Oh, yeah. Just don't hang out over the railing too far."

He opened the door, a strong breeze blew through. "Go on out but hold the railing. After we get a look at the action, I'll help you serve all that food you've prepared."

Stephanie tapped on the glass. Joel waved her forward.

"Glad you came out, Stephanie. You'll see an interesting close-up of nature at its best. Just be careful, sometimes the boat will take an unexpected roll, so keep one hand tight on the railing as you move forward." The warm breeze whipped through the girls' hair as they stepped outside.

Tracy's long hair covered her face. Stephanie said, "Look down, Tracy. They're racing with us. I think that one's looking at us. Look how big his eyes are."

Joel encouraged them to step to the bow for a different feeling as the ship's bow rose and fell with the ocean swell. he looked back at the bridge. "Okay, girls, enough. Let's see if we can feed the hungry captain. He looks dead on his feet."

Tracy looked up at Mike slumped back in the captain's chair. The enclosed bridge, separated from the salon by a plate glass window and wet bar, allowed him to watch the activity at both ends of the ship. She knew he longed for a little rest. She caught Joel's eye. "Let's go feed the tiger."

"How's it shaping up out there, pard?" Mike said.

"Everything's good so far. That's some feast the girls have laid out. I checked below decks before coming up. You should consider yourself relieved and get stoked up for a good rest, tired old friend. I can keep one eye on everything here while we grab a bite, it looks delicious."

"That's good, Joel. Can you handle things until midnight? Maybe set the girls up with a two-hour relief watch during the middle of our eight hours. It'll keep us awake and provide a pee break. Of course, one of us will always be sacked out here in the sea cabin. I'm dead tired. It's up to you to brief them on everything."

Tracy grabbed his arm. "Come with me, sad sack. You need nourishment and a good rest."

Joel dipped his head. "I've got the bridge, go ahead and grab a bite."

"Got a lot on my mind," Mike said. "We should put our heads together and figure out what we're going to do with those two canvas bags. And how we plan to handle the unavoidable check-in with the authorities in San Diego?"

Tracy pushed him toward the salon where a delightful meal was set out.

He said, "Hi, Stephanie. You're beautiful! How did you do it after all you've been through?"

She hugged him. "You're just a big sweet talker, Mike. Besides. Tracy has always been the beauty of our family."

The meal ended and Tracy held onto Mike. She felt anxious. "Please, Mike. I'm having trouble forgetting

Hondo's body lying there on the deck. And then there was Turk. I'm concerned about you and Joel being in trouble, nothing more. Are you going to have a serious problem with it? Those two were violent predators and deserved everything that happened to them."

"Listen to me," he said. "This may upset you more, but everything will be okay. I'm tired right now and may not be thinking straight. Here's what we have to deal with. First there's the matter of the unavoidable death of two members of a violent drug cartel, as you pointed out. Next, there's the uncertainty of not knowing if we've been identified by Lance Howell, a leader with this violent cartel. Third. It was necessary to dispose of a million-dollar vessel to prevent any association or connection to those of us here, with those violent deaths."

"I know, Mike. I'm trying to process it all."

He looked at her before continuing. "And fourth. There's something that may make it easier to swallow. It's quite possible that both of you may have become wealthy as a result of your ordeal."

She puzzled over his statement. She opened her mouth to speak.

"Hold on! I'll explain in a moment. One more thing. It's most important. We must present a plausible story to the authorities as we check back into the United States. Our story will be looked carefully because we need to turn over those recovered handbags. That's something, my dear, that needs to be thoroughly investigated. As for the death of two violent killers. My conscience doesn't bother me at all. The possibility of wealth…"

He signaled Joel. "Would you mind bringing up those two canvas bags?

"Now, Tracy. You can see we're all in this predicament together. There's a great deal of money in those bags Joel's bringing up. You and Stefanie should take it someplace quiet, maybe into the unused dining room, and count it. I believe that cash is in bundles. If so, note the denominations, then count each bundle to assure accuracy."

She became confused, even more worried. "Mike. I don't understand. Doesn't this just complicate the problem?"

"Maybe not. Everything has to be handled in a proper manner."

She can tell, he's patient, trying to explain everything for her benefit. "I'm only concerned about you getting in serious trouble. You've done so much for Steph and me."

"I don't want to say, 'trust me' and then disappoint you. I believe everything will work out. Let me handle things. I'm sorry if all this makes you more uncertain."

He looked at the faces staring at him. "Now, for the money. Make a notation on one sheet of paper only. We don't want any kind of evidence left around to create questions.

He stood up. "I'm going down and try to sleep for six or seven hours. If I don't get some rest, that mid-watch is going to be hell on high water."

"I don't know what to say, Mike. Nothing like this could be happening to us. Stephanie and I are ordinary boring people. Won't all that money just complicate our problem more?"

Chapter 10

Ladies' man, Lance Howell struggled to rise off the piss covered floor, his blue eyes and blond hair filled with his own blood. He yelled to his henchmen. "Get those damned women in the van and tie them up good. Now, before that bastard tries to interfere again! And get me some help here. I'm hurt. I'm going to kill that big bastard."

The women tried to hide in the ladies' room, pleading with a Caucasian patron. "Help us! Men out there tried to force us to go with them," screamed the tall woman with one eye swollen shut.

"Is there an exit out the rear?" said the other. "These men want to kidnap us, maybe kill us. Please, we're all alone here."

Startled, the young woman at the mirror turned toward the rear cubicle to answer. She was grabbed and violently shaken by one of the men.

Lance's hired strongmen. Brothers Hondo and Turk rushed into the ladies' room without consideration for any women who might be compromised.

Hondo held the young white female at the mirror.

Turk slammed into the stalls one after the other. He yelled out, "Got 'em!" Both men crowded into the restroom stall to subdue the two women.

The tall dark-haired woman kicked and fought violently. She landed a hard kick to Turk's crotch. He cursed loudly in Spanish and backed out of the cubicle.

Hondo saw the damage to his brother and slammed an elbow hard into the woman's face, that knocked her back against the wall. Within minutes, both women were dragged outside through a side door, shoved into an old Ford van and tied to seats behind the driver. Still fighting, they were taken to a dirty little warehouse near the marina to be locked in a small dark room with one bare mattress on a rusty bed frame. A tiny cubicle in the corner provided a commode and sink.

Turk said. "I'd like to kick the shit out o' that big woman. I don't care how much she's worth. My nuts hurt."

"Lance would kill you. This is business to him, and his orders were clear. Don't damage the goods! You know we get a crack at them only if his deal falls through."

"I don't know about you, big brother. But I've had enough of Lance's dirty work. One more year of his shit and I can kick back with all the women I want."

"You ain't going nowhere and you know it. The money's too good. Now take a look around outside. We can't go aboard the boat until the whole damn marina's asleep."

Frightened and battered, the two women sat on a dirty mattress, holding each other.

Stephanie said, "I'm sorry I got you involved in this mess. You've always been there to bail me out of trouble. Now if something happens to both of us, it'll kill Mom and Dad."

"We can't think like that, damn it. This toilet tissue is soaked with blood. Will you see if there's any by the toilet? My nose won't stop bleeding."

Stephanie answered, "Shit, shit, shit. There's no paper and there's not even a seat on this filthy toilet. I have to pee so bad my knees are shaking."

"Just spread your legs and go anyway. Don't waste a thought about going on the floor. At least we can't see the bugs in here without lights."

Hours later, Hondo opened the door. He flashed a bright light directly into the faces of the frightened women. "You come easy, I'll only tie your hands in front. You act up, I'll stuff your underwear in your mouth and put a hood over your head. What's it going-ta-be?"

"We'll go along quietly if you'll treat us properly. We're tired, hungry and I need first aid treatment."

Howell operated a fleet of feeder vessels that rendezvoused with freighters transporting cartel drugs and human cargo. Small panga boats were pre-loaded and dropped at various points along the California coast.

Lance shouted at his assistant, Augustine Palmyra, standing in the main office at Port San Quintin. "I'm hospitalized in Cabo with serious injuries. The payment for that last shipment is past-due. Listen up, August. I want you to get hold of the Guerrero brothers as soon as possible. They should be back aboard my yacht in Cabo by now, with some very valuable cargo that's to be offered up through the usual channels. Have them call my cell number in exactly two hours. I'm doing everything possible to get out of this fucking hospital. I can talk business with them when I have the privacy of my own vehicle. Make damn sure they keep trying to reach me."

Later, he answered the phone from his SUV. He bellowed into his cell, "God damn it, Hondo, you heard what I said. You and Turk are going to have to take full responsibility for this trip. You've made it with me often enough to handle it right, and that means absolutely no screw ups. You have the payoff money onboard and your expense money. I expect my yacht to be returned in the same shape it's in now — excellent. Don't let that half-million-dollar payment for the shippers tempt you."

Hondo growled. "Boss, I don't want to do this. That's a big ocean. I might not be able to find the island."

"I showed you how to use the GPS multiple times. You've taken the boat out four or five times with me along. You didn't need my help. You're being paid well. So don't give me any crap. My penalty for betrayal is painful before you die. Listen carefully now. I'm going to say it one more time. The women are to be fed and cared for without more brutality. They may prove very valuable. Until I'm sure of the deal, you're responsible for their well-being. It's possible that you'll have to dispose of them at sea if the sale doesn't work out. You have all the waypoint information for the rendezvous? Yes, there in the pilot house. Yes. Again, if disposal is necessary, you may have them as you like. Then wrap the bodies in chain and dump them in deep water far from land. Do not move in that direction until I tell you to."

Lance's yacht, *Sly Fox,* traveled all day on a course of 330 degrees, with moderate winds and a five-foot swell out of the west. The powerful sport fisher sliced through the seas with ease. Not so for the women locked in a small stateroom.

Hondo instructed Turk, "Go see to the women. If they agree to my terms and cause no problems, let them into the galley and salon. You keep your pants zipped up. We have plenty of time for that."

Turk unlocked the door of the starboard guest suite where the sisters were fighting nausea and fear of the unknown. He looked down at the tall woman. "We may allow you into the galley and salon. First you agree to make coffee, sandwiches and help us when we ask. Most important, you cause no problems and follow orders at once. You agree?"

"Do we have any other choice?"

"Not unless you want to be locked in this room for many days. We'll be meeting with other men in thirty-six hours. You'll have freedom of the boat until then. But you must stay quiet in your room when the men come aboard. You understand?"

"We'll do what you say and cause no trouble as long as you don't try to hurt us."

Chapter 11

Dr Figueroa slammed his medical bag down. "Lance, you're leaving the hospital too soon. I've done everything I can for you. Follow my instructions. Keep the stitching clean, dry, and continue treating with antibiotic cream, or you'll have noticeable scarring on your face. The broken ribs will also give you more trouble than you expect without proper treatment. I advise you to stay here a couple more days to be on the safe side."

"No, Doc! I'm trying to run a business. I've got a lot in play right now. Got to get back to work. You sign the damn release slip. I'm out of here."

"You paid for my service, now take my advice. Limit your activity for the next few weeks."

Lance felt the blast of humid air outside. *Sonofabitch! Damn all big muscle-bound assholes as well as this frigging weather. That goes for half of all the people I know.*

"August, what'd you find out about the bastard that blindsided me in the toilet?"

"I have several people working on it. You're going to need patience on this. We haven't got much to go on. Word is, he had to be a truck driver operating in and out of the port there in Cabo. He fit the description of several big men operating from California or Arizona. Forget about that guy for now, Lance. He'll show up again and then we'll nail him."

"To hell with you, August. It's not your face the bastard busted up. I've got it all set up with a few of our people. Once we locate him, I'll cut him up good."

"Frankly, I don't trust the Guerreros to handle things around Guadalupe, chief. This is one of the largest deliveries we've ever organized, and we should concentrate on getting it finalized before something or someone screws it up."

"You're right, of course. Those two turds grabbed my personal yacht and a pot full of cash. One more thing, August. They have two of the best-looking women I've ever seen locked up on board waiting for me to work out a deal through our Middle Eastern brokers. Those babes should bring a record-breaking price. Now, let's get home so we can keep tabs on the Guerrero boys. They had better not screw this thing up."

Augustine rushed back into Lance's air-conditioned office above the warehouse floor. "One of the trawler captains just came in, boss. He said he was present aboard your yacht last night for the transfer of funds. It appeared, to have gone anyway but good. Furthermore, the ship's people are hesitant to do more business until final payment for this deal is made. They're demanding your presence on any future business. Would you care to fill me in?"

"The fucking ship's captain demanded an extra twenty-five-grand for himself at the rendezvous. I ordered the Guerrero brothers to deliver only fifty percent of what's owed until the ship's owners can be contacted. Those were my instructions, August."

Lance scratched at his crotch. "Some of the boys are getting greedy. We can't let them think we're losing control or things will get out of hand. The Guerrero boys have another meeting on the seventeenth for final payment. They're to return here immediately after the meeting. They also have the full half-million in cash on board. No one else is aware of that, August. Let's hope it stays that way."

Both men sat in front of an array of high-tech satellite communications equipment in Lance's office.

"My last conversation with Hondo was at eleven-thirty last night," Lance said. "Everything was on schedule for an afternoon meeting confirmed with the ship's representative for two-thirty this afternoon. The asshole was supposed to call me at eight sharp this morning to check in. I've called the yacht every thirty minutes since then and still get no response. We don't have any other boats in the area, do we?"

"No. Port San Quentin is the closest mainland seaport within range. There's not another load planned from here until July twenty-second. The long-range trawlers are fishing south of here during down time. I've a bad feeling about this. We have too much at stake here to play around pretending it hasn't happened, boss."

"Remember, August. Those two could've been tempted by the half-million in cash. It makes me think we've been taken.

"Don't you think you should put out an alert for your yacht?"

"Damn it to hell, August. Our only help here is going to come from our own initiative and our own people. Get in touch with the trawler skippers and see what they know." Still fuming, he slammed his fist down.

Augustine moved back. "Is that all you need from Me?"

"Hell no! Here's what I want you to do after talking with the skippers. Get out to the nearest airport that offers charters and hire something with enough range to search the area around Guadalupe Island first. If they were there at nine-thirty last night, then a plane search will locate the bastards. You know what? I don't know for sure that's where they were at that time. If they planned to take the money and run, they had time to get almost anywhere. Hell, we don't know for sure that something's wrong. Shit! We don't know anything, do we?"

"Well, boss. I still think it's a good bet that we start looking now. We can cancel everything quickly if you hear from them. I never trusted those two anyway."

"Stay in touch, August. I'll call you if I reach them. Meanwhile. I'm alerting all of our contacts here and in the U.S. to be on the lookout for *Sly Fox* and the Guerrero brothers." *I'm not about to let August or anyone else know there's over a million dollars of my own money hidden aboard the Sly Fox, on top of the half-million owed to the shipping outfit.*

.

Augustine returned to Lance's office from the cubby hole in the warehouse where he conducted his cartel business. "Lance! I've exhausted all possibilities except one. There's an expatriate American in La Paz who has a twin-engine Seneca with a five-hundred-mile range. This guy's name is Mark Wynn and the airplane is in San Jose Viejo today. He'll be back in La Paz tomorrow morning. The earliest he can be airborne is eleven a.m. tomorrow, the eighteenth. He's asking for a five-thousand-dollar deposit up front to take off."

"Okay, August. I can't take to the air myself. You go along and stay in touch with me here at the office. I don't plan to leave until this situation is worked out. I've been in touch with the ship's representative and I'll know for sure about the Guerrero boys by this afternoon at rendezvous time. I'll let you know then. It was necessary to guarantee full payment to the owners regardless of today's outcome. The situation with the captain will be taken care of by their organization."

He grabbed an arm. "August, I'm giving you enough cash to keep that plane in the air until we locate the *Sly Fox*. You know how we operate. I'll need an accounting of every dollar. Get that plane in the air as soon as you can tomorrow. We know there's a good chance those guys planned to run with the cash right after the first meeting on June fourteenth. If that's true, they could be as far as a thousand miles from the rendezvous point near Guadalupe Island. Start your air search from La Paz down around the shoreline to Cabo and back up, checking all potential ports of call where fuel and supplies could be purchased. At Isla Cerros, fly directly out to Guadalupe and take a close look at all the coves where *Sly Fox* could be hiding."

Augustine stopped Lance. "This is going to be time consuming. Couldn't it wait?"

"Hell no! Return to the mainland and continue north all the way to the border area. Don't forget to look around any of the offshore islands such as the Coronados. Work with the pilot as necessary to plan your fuel stops. I seriously doubt they'd cross the border into the US. If we don't locate the *Sly Fox* with this air search, I'm afraid the escape plan may have taken them across to Mazatlán. I plan to alert our contacts as far south as Guatemala."

Those thieving bastards have stolen my boat, found my personal funds in the bed and ran. The value of the boat and cash aboard, nearly three million dollars lost. Enough to tempt Father Murphy himself. Got to find that boat.

Lance was dangerous to be around. Workers preparing the next shipment avoided him. He turned from his desk, kicked the trash can across the room. He called Maria from her desk outside. "Get Capitan Mendez in here as soon as he's back in port." *My best man flying all over Mexico instead of directing the workers and stockpiling product at the warehouse.*

He leaned over his desk, agonized over the last few days. Everything was going fine until that big bastard interfered. I'm going to kill him. First, he has to know who I am and suffer ten times as much pain as he caused me. It's his fault these shipments are in jeopardy.

Lance looked at his watch, and realized time was short. He knew he'd better get the operation back on track. He picked up the phone and punched in a number. "August, this is Lance. Call me when you're back on the ground."

Chapter 12
2010 Tuscaloosa Alabama

Mike McGowin slid his feet off the coffee table, stretched, and tossed down the *Sports Illustrated* magazine. The article had praised him for his outstanding play at linebacker. "Hey, pal, are we partying tonight?" Damn, he loved this place, the violence of playing big-time college football, proud of his aggressive reputation for the Crimson Tide.

Bill nodded. "So, Mike. No more 'Bama football. No more painkillers, wind sprints, or two-a-day practice sessions. The U.S. Army might have you longing to be back in the game."

"Nah, Bill! Been there, done that, enjoyed every minute. I'm anxious to take a new direction with my life. Got a lot of catching up to do."

"Yeah! Let's go get cleaned up. Can't keep the ladies waiting ya know." He looked at Mike with a grin. "You behave yourself around my favorite girl tonight. Someday you have to give me your secret for charming the beauties."

"Come on, Bill, you do all right. I'm really gonna miss you. Best roommate ever."

"You haven't packed up your dinner jacket, have you? In all that stuff you've stored away in your closets?"

"I pulled it out and cleaned it up after your invite. I finally get to use some of that crap Mom forced on me. Never unpacked most of it. I told her 'Bama football didn't leave time for many outside activities. You know, Bill. Mom's the reason we share this apartment. I think she realized it'd take a big place to store all this useless stuff. A quiet place to study was secondary to her. She was a party girl in her college days."

Mike dressed in a dark dinner jacket with a pleated shirt, white gold and black studs, matching cuff links and light gray slacks. Damn! He looked good.

"Hey, Bill. You ready? I am. Do I have to wear the bow tie if I'm not going to the ball?"

"Open collar with dinner jacket's okay for the cocktail party. Son-of-a-gun, Mike, for a big bad ass, you clean up nice. I may have to change my mind about letting you meet Casey."

Mike studied his pal. Bill had no idea how good he looked. Damn good friend too. "Do you suppose we can walk the three blocks to the Phi-Kappa-Sigma house without freezing our asses off? I could really use the exercise."

"Feel free to walk, big guy. I need my car. I'm taking Casey straight to the ballroom after the cocktail party."

Mike had an easy jog to the frat house. He found Bill talking to friends inside the front door, who led Mike to the coat check girl. She said, "Hi, handsome," and tossed the coat onto a full table.

He looked around. Was impressed. A large white Christmas tree, then a brightly decorated main dining room and roaring fire in a stone fireplace. Smartly dressed servers passed through the crowd with trays of glistening champagne and delicious looking hors d'oeuvres.

Bill drifted into the crowd, greeted friends and fraternity brothers.

A head taller than anyone else, he looked out over the sea of happy people, enjoying the mixture of Christmas carols and easy listening jazz heard above the laughter and tinkling of glasses. He grabbed a second glass of champagne, fascinated with a tall dark-haired girl holding a champagne glass. She talked with a man near the fireplace. Her deep throated laugh stimulated his interest. He headed in her direction until someone grabbed his shoulder.

"Mike, I thought you accepted that Forty-Niner offer and bailed."

"No, Charley, that was a decent offer but not in my plans for the future."

"I read you're not entering the draft but I don't believe it."

"Yeah, I have a couple of years obligated to Uncle Sam before making permanent plans. Say, Charley.

Who's that tall brunette with the long legs standing near the Christmas tree?"

"I don't know, Mike. Long legs go with short skirts. She's certainly attractive, with a Delta Zeta pin on that beautiful chest. Someone said she's from Las Vegas, maybe a show girl."

"Shit, Charley. I think I'm falling in love. Maybe I've been living with the animals too long. You don't suppose I'll have to kill her friend if I mosey over and talk to her, do you?"

Charley laughed. "Nah, don't rush it. You'll know everybody here within an hour."

Chapter 13
2010

Tracy Conwell moved around the crowded room. She accepted a glass of bubbly, admired the well-dressed group of people. A whole week here with Cathy. She couldn't wait. Last week had been hard. Hell, all last month was hard. The last game against sister program Nevada, horrible, lost big. She wanted some excitement. She moved around near the big fireplace, enjoyed talking sports with several interesting men. Ben started talking about legal briefs. Boring. She saw Cathy waving her over, said, "Excuse me, Ben." She weaved her way through the crowd to stop near Cathy.

Cathy grabbed her hand. "Mike, I want you to meet my cousin, Tracy. She's a jock like you, only prettier. Anyway, we grew up together in Las Vegas. He's a cocky bastard, Tracy. But lovable when on good behavior." She gave Mike a hard look. "Don't let his schoolboy charm get you. Mike, you look after Tracy. Ben and I are leaving early for the formal dance at the Hilton."

Tracy was curious about this guy. She'd caught him looking a few times. Too good looking, probably all into himself. "So, Mike. I've never been to a formal affair like this before. Is it a usual thing here?"

"Most of the Greek clubs have at least one formal cocktail party, followed by a formal dance at one of the hotel ballrooms. Usually held during the fall semester, around the holidays."

She swallowed the last of the bubbly. "Well! How long have you known Cathy?"

He looked at her. "We were pretty close our sophomore year. She claimed I only wanted help with my chemistry class.

Mike grabbed a couple glasses of champagne from a passing server. He passed one to Tracy.

She grinned. "You look like you might play basketball."

"No, but I'm pretty good at pocket pool and sometimes I win at dodgeball."

"Now I know who you are. Mike McGowin, the bone breaking linebacker all the pro teams are talking about. You're holding out for more money."

"Not for more money. I made a firm commitment to the army. Then, there's the family corporation."

I read the sports pages. What's up with this guy?

She touched his arm, feeling a bit reckless, "I can't imagine a guy your age turning down a multi-million-dollar contract. Was it because Daddy said come home?"

"I loved playing football at Alabama but I'm anxious to be more productive. After the army, I want to build things with my hands and mind."

Tracy's antenna quivered. *Is this guy for real?*

She touched his arm again. "Let's move farther away from the fire." She stopped near the over-decorated Christmas tree. They talked about other athletes and a few mutual friends. She sensed he was trying to behave, not too forward. He held her arm when they moved around, made eye contact. *Interested.*

She looked into his eyes. "Mike, you're not with someone, are you?"

Mike smiled and shook his head.

Tracy added, "I'm not used to drinking. Would I be too forward by suggesting a bite to eat somewhere the music isn't too loud? This fine champagne could upset the apple cart if I'm not careful."

"No. I would be delighted. I know just the place. I'll let Cathy know. She must have her cell phone."

She thought, *So easy to fall for this big guy. He seems interested in everything about me. He just wants to score.*

Bill Campbell returned with his friend. He introduced himself to Tracy. "And this is my friend, Casey," he said, and she immediately turned to Mike.

"And you must be Mike, the roommate that's never there. Bill has spoken so highly of you."

Tracey turned awkwardly to avoid Mike's foot. She lost her balance, caused both to fall toward the brightly lit Christmas tree. Barely avoided a catastrophe. *Damn champagne.*

Mike quickly pulled her in tight against his chest. He turned quickly to fall with his back to the floor. After a moment, he placed a hand to each side of Tracy's face and tenderly kissed her soft lips.

Standing nearby, Casey said, "Oh my God, Tracy! Are you hurt?"

Bill quickly reached down and pulled Tracy to her feet.

On unsteady legs, she said, "No! I'm not hurt, just embarrassed, and a little damp." Her laugh set the tone for those gathered around. "I'm fine. I was just careless."

Mike said, "Should I wait for you here while you're in the ladies' room? I'll drive you for a change of clothes."

"That would be nice. I won't be long. *" It could've been the champagne.*

Bill said, "The wine spilled down the front of her beautiful cocktail dress. She sure handles it well."

Tracy returned to Mike, smiling at their predicament. "Let's grab our coats and go for dry clothes."

"Wait! I almost forgot. My car's at the apartment. I can hoof it over and be back in a few minutes."

"Frankly, I think the walk would be great if it's not too far. My coat will be warm enough for me." She hoped her type 'A' personality wouldn't get her in trouble.

At the door, Tracey said. "Lucky dog. How the hell did a jock on an athletic scholarship manage a place like this?"

"To be honest, this place was arranged by my crazy mother through my father's alumni association. He also played football at Alabama. The deal was made well in advance of my showing up on campus. I prefer not to get into it right now if you don't mind. But I know what you were thinking."

"What was I thinking?"

"That this pad's for wild parties. I spend very little time here. Football players at Alabama don't have time for that, if they also want a decent education. I loved playing football, spent most of my time with teammates and coaching staff at the dorm. I had a room there. There were periods when I needed quiet study time. Then, this place was a blessing."

"I didn't mean it like it sounded. I know how hard you worked to be good at football. I'm just jealous. Believe me. I worked my ass off at UNLV too, as a basketball player on scholarship struggling to keep at least a 3.0 GPA. I'll be twenty-one next month, and I still live at home. So, don't let my crankiness get to you. This is my Christmas vacation and I've enjoyed your company very much."

She knew he liked looking at her in the wet clothes.

"I have an assortment of sweats and stuff if you want to try something like that. We can go casual some place."

Tracy noticed the neatly made king-size bed. She moved past two bare bureaus to stop at double closets. She moved from one closet to the other, fascinated. One was full of casual shirts, and other attire. The other, crowded with luggage, opened on luggage stands. Some were tightly packed as if ready for a long trip.

"Where does your girlfriend keep her belongings?"

"I told you. There hasn't been time for girlfriends or serious involvements in my life. Sure. I've had very casual flings but no one special."

"I know, I'm only pulling your chain some." She looked at the open drawers he'd pulled out. "May I look those over?" She pulled out several sets of sweats, spreading them on the bed.

Mike broke her concentration. "I'm going to need a pair of those for myself. I can't go dressed like this while the most beautiful girl in the world goes on the town modeling men's athletic wear."

Tracy tried on several pairs of sweats. She still looked feminine enough. She pulled her long dark hair back, formed a ponytail and secured it in place with a sweatband normally worn on the wrist. She left the pearl necklace on a bureau top. *I can't believe I'm doing this.*

She rejoined Mike. "Are you sure you don't have ladies' underwear around here someplace?"

He ignored her comment. "Wow, I can't believe what you did to my sweats! Uh-oh, no shoes. I'll check Bill's closet." He returned moments later with a pair of low-cut canvas deck shoes and a new pair of athletic socks. "Here, try these on while I get out of this wet shirt."

She watched Mike strip off the soiled shirt until he turned, nodded and closed the bedroom door, still fascinated by the wide shoulders and highly defined back muscles. She tried on the shoes. To her surprise, nearly a perfect fit. *For once big feet are good. After all, I'm five feet nine inches tall. That's as tall as some men I know.*

Mike left his bedroom dressed similarly to Tracy: running shoes, sweat pants and a plain navy colored sweatshirt. "Okay! Let's go fill that gorgeous body with some comfort food."

"Mike, you were a 'Bama athlete! Don't you want to wear the 'Bama colors? You have several nice workout suits in the bedroom."

"No. Not now," he said. "I'm a soon to be forgotten college athlete and prefer to look ahead toward the future, not behind. Maybe it's a dread of the unknown. I don't know why I feel that way. It just seems less important to me now."

She watched him walk to the closet and select two hooded jackets and toss one to her.

"Hey! I know a place for a good late-night steak. How does that sound?"

He opened the passenger door of a five-year-old BMW sedan, one hand on Tracy's elbow.

"Gee, Mike, you're a constant surprise."

Twenty minutes later, they pulled off the two-lane highway. "Roadhouse," Tracy said, reading the bright sign over a large log structure placed back beneath huge pine trees. There were half a dozen cars and several pickup trucks, most parked in front of the brightly decorated restaurant.

Mike opened a heavy wooden door. They passed through a small mud room, into a warm, well decorated dining room. The dance floor was surrounded by padded oval shaped booths across from a well-stocked bar. She looked around, then hesitated. "Look, Mike. Another beautiful Christmas tree for us to fall into."

Mike laughed. "You know darn well that fall was contrived just so I could pull you close and kiss you."

"You're impressed with yourself, aren't you, Mr Linebacker? That kiss did seem kind of special. *" Why did I say that? Can't let him know.*

Mike reached across the table, touched her hand lightly. "Someday you're going to be the mother of my children. You know that don't you?"

"Like hell I am." She pulled her hand away. "Arrogance gets you nowhere. Maybe that kiss wasn't so special."

"Saved by the bell," he said.

An attractive older woman stepped up to take their order.

"What would you folks like to drink?"

Mike looked at Tracy. "Does a glass of Syrah sound okay to you, or would you like something different?"

"That would be nice as long as we order soon." *Be careful now, one more might be over the edge.*

He looked at the waitress. "Give us a bottle of your best Syrah and let us look over a menu as soon as possible. This poor waif has been wandering the hinterlands without proper nourishment."

She glared at Mike. "You! Smart ass. All the way here your stomach made noises like my old Volkswagen climbing a hill." *He just ordered a bottle, not a glass. I'm okay, I think.*

Returning with the wine, the friendly waitress said, "The filet mignon is particularly good this evening, as well as the New York."

Tracy spoke first. "The filet sounds good to me, with all the trimmings. Mike? Medium rare?"

"Medium rare, but I'll have the New York the same way with all the trimmings."

Throughout the meal, she thought of that tender kiss. She asked more personal questions. They were answered. She became more aware of his tenderness. *Why can't I meet this most perfect man on my own home base? I'm not interested in a short-term romance.* "Dance with me, Mike!"

He led her onto the dance floor.

"It must be the music," she said. "I've never felt so mellow. The soft tunes are wonderful." She placed one hand on his shoulder and gently toyed with the hair at his neckline. Soon other couples joined them on the floor.

"I'm enjoying myself immensely. You must have concerns about me. A strange girl in a strange town, with a strange man."

"No! I believe we all have dreams where suddenly that special person appears out of nowhere and fulfills that dream. I certainly think about it. And, you are the most attractive and interesting woman I have ever known."

"It just hasn't happened with me. Am I only imagining that those things happen to people like me?"

"I see you as patiently preparing yourself for all kinds of opportunities yet to come."

How in hell did he pick up on that?

They spent more and more time on the dance floor. She enjoyed his gentle strength while in his arms. The wine bottles were empty, the dining room closed. *What am I doing? I've never been this forward in all my life.*

The band packed up to go home. "Mike, the music has stopped. Shouldn't we leave the dance floor?"

He lifted her face tenderly, looking into her eyes. "We can't allow this evening to end so soon. I've finally found someone I can care for. Where in the world have you been hiding all my life?"

"I don't know, Mike. I'm afraid that kiss meant much more than I wish to admit. I've never had this problem before." *This better be a dream.*

On the drive back to his apartment Tracy said, "I don't know what to do. I'm not prepared to stay overnight. I want very much to be with you, but what should I do?" *I know what I should do. I'm old enough to know better, maybe too young to resist this guy.*

Mike removed his hand from Tracy's knee, rubbed it over the five o'clock shadow now evident on his face. "You must see Cathy tomorrow for sure. Are you willing to rough it with me until then? Your beautiful cocktail dress will be dry. Or, we can get you some casual clothes as soon as the stores open. I can afford it."

She was impressed with his warmth and sincerity. Different from anyone she'd ever known.

Mike said, "Let's do this. Tomorrow morning, at a decent hour, call Cathy to let her know that we're shopping. Tell her what your plans are beyond that."

"I think that might work. Are you sure about shopping on my behalf? Please don't make me feel like I traded a bit of myself for a few items of clothing. This is all new to me. I'm very unsure of myself right now." *I hope like hell I'm doing the right thing.*

Back at Mike's apartment, she said, "I'm not accustomed to sleeping bare. Do you mind if I snoop around in your stuff a little more? Moments later she held up a large, short sleeved T-shirt with USC printed on the back. "Ha, you traitor! look what you were hiding."

Mike smiled. "I once thought that might be my team. I visited Alabama and was sold on the sincerity, dedication to football and friendliness of everyone I met."

Mike lightly touched her lips with his. She responded with the tip of her tongue. They explored each other's body. Soon passionate kissing chafed Tracy's face, she was beyond caring. Their tongues touched and tangled lightly at first, then moved furiously as Mike held one breast, then the other.

"Now, Mike. Show me now, please." She reacted with a soft intake of breath, then relaxed, to let him know that everything was going well.

Mike hesitated. He realized Tracy was a virgin. He forced himself to remain still for a moment. He removed his lips from Tracy's. "You're still a virgin, Tracy. Why didn't you tell me?"

"Would it make a difference, Mike? Please go ahead. I want you so much!"

Later, she was aware of a new found closeness, lying together. The warm tender feeling she had for him had grown into a white-hot emotional flame. She didn't know what to make of it all. She wiped a single tear from her cheek.

Mike was quiet. He placed his lips on her cheek. "I'm very much afraid. You've grown far too important to me, Tracy. My life's course has been charted across the world and you'll be so far away."

"Yes, Mike, I know. We're going to be very special to each other unless, life gets in the way before we have a chance to live."

Chapter 14

The U.S. Military reentered Afghanistan in 2008 as Stage III of America's longest war in history. In 2014 Major Mike McGowin was recalled to his old Army intelligence unit.

The exploding rocket took out the sentry hut at the south entrance of the walled compound. Automatic weapons fire raked the building through the opening. Colonel Findley grabbed his boots. "What's the situation, Lieutenant?"

He was concerned. The Afghan Allies responsible for protecting the small outpost had proven themselves to be undisciplined.

"They've breached the wall in two places, sir. It looks bad. Our own people have driven the RPG team back with very accurate small arms fire. The enemy has a small attack force with automatic weapons at both locations."

"Hot damn. We don't have enough of our team here for protection. Give me what's available of a rifle team.

I'll head for the breach at the south entrance. Rally our people at the second breach."

A mile away, Major McGowin, Staff Sergeant Sid Goddard and their interpreter Peg, a man with a metal alloy leg, were camped in the mountains near a small village. They'd assisted the villagers throughout the night trying to prevent a small reservoir dam from collapsing. Heavy rains had flooded over the dam near a concrete spillway. The small lake was a primary source of water for the mountain community. Using heavy stone, sand-bags and a great deal of manual labor, soft earthen sections near the overflowing spillway were reinforced. The critical period had passed.

"Let's go, home Sergeant. I could use about a gallon of coffee and a bucket of bacon and eggs. With the rain gone and the sun coming up, I believe these folks will be able to finish the job without us."

"They should continue with rock reinforcements all the way around, Major. Otherwise, the next heavy rain may just spread the problem out further. I'll have Peg keep track of their progress."

"That works for me, Sid. Call in Peg, set it up. Let's make tracks."

They approached the Humvee. Private Hill, the radio operator, shouted over loud yelling from Andy Fagan at headquarters.

"Major McGowin. Hold up, sir. This is an emergency!"

"We were hit hard about two hours ago, Major. A group of well-armed insurgents blew right past the Afghan security force to attack the poorly defended headquarters building. Colonel Findley led a counter-attack against the penetrating force. He was injured and taken prisoner during the attack. A group of five or six attackers broke away dragging the colonel with them. We exchanged fire another forty minutes. The accuracy of our men took a high toll on the enemy before they withdrew into the mountains. Sergeant Moore and the sniper team left with two interpreters to plan a rescue. They're counting on your help."

"I understand, Lieutenant. Have one man pack enough rations and extra ammunition for our weapons. Have him meet us at grid point 70134211. Sergeant Goddard, Peg and me will relieve him of his load there and hike into the mountains behind the sniper team. A two-day supply should be enough. You're now in charge. Reorganize the Afghan security force, keeping the head shed well informed. Let them know that I believe a larger force on the scene might result in the insurgents killing the colonel. No helicopters in the air unless called. Now put me in touch with the sniper team. Oh, one more thing, did Sergeant Moore take both scoped 50-CAL. weapons?"

"No, Major. He elected to take one of the new M107 semi-auto weapons. He wanted to travel light and move fast. He did take two M24 scoped 7.62 weapons. The rest of the team is carrying M14 carbines."

"Good! Send the heavy 50-CAL weapon with six mags and another scoped-up M24 with nine mags. We'll leave the two M4 carbines we have with us. We're going to have a heavy load going up those mountains. Sergeant Godard, Peg and I'll be waiting at grid point 70134211."

Sergeant Moore, with five other well trained riflemen and their two well-armed Afghan interpreters pursued the enemy over the first high mountain ridge, overlooking a narrow valley. They stopped and studied both the valley and high mountain trails through their magnified rifle scopes. He saw several trails leading down the mountain from a stone defensive position about 1200 meters up, near the summit. Remnants of some long-ago outpost.

McGowin reached for the radio.

"Sergeant Dick Moore here, Major. We've located the group holding the injured Colonel Findley."

"Copy that. Now fill me in, Dick."

"There are a small group of six insurgents holding the colonel. They're holed up in a small rock outcropping about 800 meters ahead of us, Major. We have good eyes on all six. We're attempting to slip in another hundred meters closer before starting the dance."

"That's good, Dick. If they attempt to move out, can you stop them without getting the colonel killed?

I'm afraid they're slowing to arrange a transfer of the prisoner."

"That may be the case. We think we've located some kind of defensive position much higher up the mountain. That could be their destination. From our current location we should be able to take out those holding the colonel if they attempt to move up the hill. We'll drive the others to cover once they expose themselves."

"That's a desperate measure, Dick. But I believe we should take it. We can be at your position within the next hour unless we run into something unexpected. If it's at all possible, separate the insurgents from our man and protect him at all cost. Pick the bastards off one at a time and flood the rocks around them with M14 fire once the ball starts."

Little over an hour later, Mike and his team approached the sniper team's position. The first loud explosion rocked the hillside, a 50-CAL sniper weapon. It was followed right away by a second shot from the heavy gun.

Mike yelled, "We may miss the action boys. Let's hurry on over the ridge. They may need us."

Sid Goddard answered, "Hell, Major. Drop that extra gear for us and hump it to the top with the 50-CAL? You won't need more than three or four mags until we get there."

"Thanks, Sid. Here, you guys divide this ammo up and catch me over the hill. If you find my carcass along the way, just kick some rocks over it."

Mike reached the crest of the hill. He had a clear view of everything going on. The sniper team had separated into two groups of four, about 250 meters apart. They held good defensive positions, keeping the insurgents pinned down in a clump of rocks. Two dead insurgents and what must be their wounded man were lying on the sloping trail just beyond a small circle of brush and rocks. He looked through the rifle scope at the enemy's small defensive position on the mountain above. He made several small adjustments to the scope, then spotted a larger force of fourteen or fifteen men cautiously moving down a mountain trail higher up.

Mike called Dick Moore. "Bad news, Dick. Look up the mountain. There are about fifteen new participants about to join the fracas. I'll stay here and set up the other 50-CAL. I'll keep an eye on the colonel and you boys as well. I'm sending Sid Goddard and Peg down the hill into effective range for their M4s. We'll have your back. The new fighters will try to encircle your position once down the mountain. From here, I can discourage the encirclement. Let's put the big 50 to work, Dick. See if you can finish off the original rat pack."

"There are only three left from that group, Major. They've gone deep. I'd like to grab the colonel now while those three are quiet, before the new boys arrive. I'm afraid he may bleed out if we delay."

"Okay, Dick. Light up the area where they're located so I can see exactly where to place my fire."

"They still have a couple of rockets, Major. I'm a little worried about having them waste one on the colonel in our rescue attempt, unless we kill all three. Fire in the hole, Major!"

Dick Moore placed four successive heavy rounds into the rocks where he believed the insurgents were holed up. It became obvious to Mike that the enemy gunmen were flattened out beyond a low outcropping of rocks. From his high position on the mountain, Mike studied the area through his scope. He lined up on the man he could see, held a deep breath, and squeezed the trigger. Another man exposed himself. He fired again, moving fast to line up the heavy weapon. He attempted to find the third man, then lowered the muzzle.

"We have a rabbit running for the weapons. Do you have him?" The other heavy weapon vibrated the hillside.

"Your shot took his leg off, Dick. That was an excellent shot on a moving target. I can finish it for the poor bastard. I believe I saw a fourth man run out with an RPG.

"Thanks for the help, Major. One of us will see about Colonel Findley. He's alive but seems to be in bad shape. I believe the fourth man made it over the ridge."

"Hold on. Your team on the right has trouble higher up on their right flank. Our heavy weapons may make a difference. It looks like about six of the dirt bags up there."

Dick asked, "Have you located the rest of their bunch?"

"Yes. I make out a total of six more, three to a group, following a trail down in front of you. Can you see them?"

Dick answered, "They're breaking into the clear without much protection. We can handle them from here. You and your boys help our guys on the flank. I'm sending a man down for the colonel."

Mike turned his attention back to the high ground where the enemy appeared to be setting up a mortar position. His location remained unknown to the enemy, well protected by huge boulders. He called Sergeant Goddard and Peg. "I suggest you two join Dick Moore and his team. Prepare for mortar fire or RPGs from the mountainside. Also, Sid, make sure the team retrieves the colonel and renders medical care at the first opportunity."

"Roger that, Major. We'll give them some help. We have eyes on the whole group."

"I'm sure you left all of our 50-CAL. ammo with me. After you join up with Dick, find out how he's faring on heavy stuff. I plan to open up on that mortar crew soon and may not have adequate ammo to get the job done. Tell everyone to make careful accurate shots when possible. Good luck down there."

The six insurgents confronting Sergeant Moore and his men must have believed themselves to be outside the range of small arms fire. A series of four shots were fired from extreme range. Scoped M24 sniper rifles in the hands of well-trained marksmen created havoc fast. Three of the enemy dropped to the ground dead or injured, before the sound could be heard. The remaining three turned back up the mountain hoping to get out of range.

Moments later, within a total time frame of seven seconds, loud explosions from the heavy 50-CAL sniper rifle echoed across the valley. The remaining three enemy combatants went down, leaving a small dust cloud rising above where they fell.

From his concealed position, Mike scoped his targets. He joined in with slow deliberate shots into the suspected mortar crew, at a distance beyond his comfortable range for accuracy. He adjusted the scope a little after each of the first two rounds, taking out three of the others in five shots. He sent the enemy into a panic, not knowing where the heavy projectiles were coming from. He continued acquiring targets, creating havoc in the rocks where the enemy sought sanctuary from heavy projectiles and rock fragments. After five long minutes without another target, he placed one round every minute into the rock formation for the next five minutes. Five rounds fired. Three remaining survivors raced in panic back across the mountain slope.

Mike recognized his own limited skill on the heavy weapon. He called Sergeant Moore. "Dick, I let three get away. They are making tracks on the mountain trail, headed back up. Are any of you free to take a few shots?"

"We can give it a try, Major. They're now almost beyond the M24 range. I want to conserve the big 50 ammo in case we have another attack."

Without waiting longer, Mike picked up his gear and headed down the mountain to check Colonel Findley's condition.

The colonel was injected with morphine and weak from loss of blood, but awake.

"Hello, Max. You look like you've been dragged through the rocks, then used for target practice. You mind if I look at that hip?" Kneeling next to the colonel, Mike could see that the bone in the man's leg had been shattered just below the pelvic socket with a small caliber through-and-through.

"Hell, Mike. I felt sure those turkeys were going to put a bullet in my head and leave me for the buzzards. The early on pain was so intense I thought I was finished anyhow."

"Yeah, Max. I hate to tell you this, but you do have a serious through-and-through. That may mean the end of your Army Reserve career. I believe you will still be an effective special agent with the FBI."

"You think it's that bad!"

"Something to be grateful for. It could have been a lot worse. You can thank Sergeant Moore for the quick pursuit and two quick accurate shots that separated you from the insurgents. I'm going to give you another shot of morphine, and then we're going home the hard way. Several miles of rough terrain down the mountain to the nearest safe evacuation point."

Mike and the team agreed to share in turns, carrying the awkward weight of the sleeping senior officer between the larger, stronger men. One man at a time would have to bear the heavy burden.

Major McGowin, being the largest man present, volunteered to make the first attempt to descend the mountain slope with their injured comrade.

Peg commented, "Sometimes being crippled has its benefits. We'll have your back, Major."

An hour into the hike down, Mike ached from the heavy load. He needed a break when Peg, 'tail end Charlie', rushed in to report they were being followed. "Major, the enemy has someone on the ridge to your left. They're hanging back out of sight.

Mike ordered his men to spread out and take up defensive positions. He said a silent prayer and continued down the mountain with his burden. He believed himself to be well beyond the reach of the enemy. He stumbled along fast as possible until rock and bullet fragments struck his lower back. He felt a stab in the back at a point just above his belt. Neither man wore body armor at this point, having given it up as being too hot and heavy. He worried about the man he carried.

Without stopping, he glanced to his left and realized one lone fighter had managed to slip around his men and fire a weapon. The man held a small caliber rifle. Before he could turn away, the man's head exploded in a cloud of brain matter. *Thank God for close friends.*

Mike continued down the mountain with his burden. He felt weak, tired and thirsty. He spotted a shady outcropping of rock and eased himself down. He wouldn't attempt to shift the position of the injured man without help. He leaned against a large boulder, relieving the weight of the man strapped to his back. He rested in the shade of the rocks knowing this might be all the rest he'd have until his injured friend could be removed from his back.

After a brief rest, he struggled to his feet, easing himself out of the shadow of the rocks. He looked around with caution before continuing down the mountain. He glanced at his compass often, praying for accurate calculations.

After another long hour of torture, he saw a dry riverbed in the distance. Not sure he could make that last four hundred meters, he forced his tired mind to dwell on his comrades in the mountains. He prayed they'd all soon arrive safely.

Thirsty and exhausted, he found a single rock in a small clearing. He hoped to be seen by his own people before the enemy could find them. He knew once he left his feet, he wouldn't be able to rise again. His last memory, a call for helicopter evacuation. The pain excruciating, he kneeled and passed out.

Chapter 15
2011 Las Vegas

Tracy Conwell finished basketball practice for the week. She hurried through a shower. She sang out, "I'm twenty-one. Tracy, you're twenty-one years old. Get your tail home." She looked at the leggy brunette in the mirror, ran her hands over the flat stomach. She stood there for several moments, thinking to herself, her eyes closed.

"Hi, Mom. What's for dinner? I'm starved."

"Sweetheart! It's your birthday, the big one. Your dad's taking us to a show at Caesar's, a dinner show."

"Wow, that's great, but can't I get a bite of something to keep my sugar level from dropping?"

"Sure. Check the fridge. Oh, got a message for you. Some guy named Mike called to wish you a happy birthday, wouldn't leave a number. He said it was an overseas call and he couldn't be reached. So, who's this Mike? I hope it's someone good for you. You haven't shown much interest in men friends lately."

"Too busy, Mom. I'll get dressed. Gotta tart up for our big dinner."

Tracy sat and stared at her reflection in the mirror. *Glad I wasn't here when he called, can't weaken now. He can't receive calls over there. Makes it easier to resist temptation.* She brushed her long dark hair again. *I should stay strong, get over this need to be with him. This sickness. Stop crying myself to sleep at night.* She moved to the closet, pulled out her favorite blouse. *Someday it'll be different, equals.*

Tracy said, "I'm surprised we didn't have to wait longer for a booth. Caesar's restaurants are usually more crowded. Can you believe it? I can drink now, legally. Even go to the clubs."

Stephanie said, "Can I have your fake ID now? All I have to do is dye my hair."

She saw Mom look at Dad. He laughed. "Sweetheart, you're twenty-one now, old enough to drink, but we don't want to hear about fake IDs or such." He looked at Stephanie and winked. "You, young lady, better be extra careful. Using a fake ID can get you in serious trouble. It's best not to go down that road."

Mom said, "Stephanie, please don't think about growing up too fast. You have plenty to do without going to clubs at your age."

"So, Tracy. Tell us about this new man in your life."

She looked at Dad, her mouth open. "Why would you think there's a man in my life?"

"Your mom and I have seen a change in you. We've talked about it and we hope it's for the best."

"I don't know. You're both too sharp for me. I didn't plan on saying anything yet. Maybe it's best, while we're all together." She looked at Steph. "Don't talk to any of our friends about this, Stephanie."

Tracy took a deep breath. She looked at her family, pushed her wine glass away. "I met the most perfect man on my visit with Cathy at the University of Alabama. Please try not to judge me, all of you. I fell in love with him even though we may never see each other again. I knew he felt the same way about me. A hopeless cause is just that, a hopeless cause."

"Honey, what's so terrible that you both can't work out any problems?"

"No Mom. Our lives went in opposite directions, already in motion when we met."

Dad said, "Go, ahead Tracy. We're all ears."

"I don't want to tell you his name yet but it's not a secret And I'm not ashamed of him. His degree's in architecture. He's serving in the Army, an officer. I hear from him a lot, but I don't call him. I allowed things to die on their own."

Mom reached for her hand. "But why! Why do this to yourself, sweetie, if you care so much?"

"Mom, you and Dad may not understand. I don't even understand myself. Call it misguided self-respect, or my fierce independence. We started out as perfect strangers at a cocktail party and never left each other's side for three days and three nights — the most wonderful time of my life. We knew beforehand the challenges of life already worked against us. I've thought about this a great deal. Fate allowed our lives to intersect for a-brief moment in time, those three days. The path of his future pointed away from mine, as if he was being pulled by some irresistible force. I didn't have the courage to intervene."

"Oh, honey, you're so hard on yourself."

"Mom, Dad. You're the most wonderful parents in the world, so. I'm going to need your help more than ever."

Tracy took a big swallow of wine and passed the glass to Stephanie. "I visited Dr Schuman today and he confirmed what I suspected. I'm pregnant with a child by a man I may never see again. Believe it or not I'm happy."

Dad got up, left the table. Mom reached across for Tracy's hand as if she were a small child.

Dad returned to the table. "So, Tracy. You don't want to marry the child's father."

"I love him a lot, Dad. Please, both of you. Let me make this decision on my own. I do pray that after a time, we will become a family. I can't do that to him at this time."

Dad sat down. "Honey, you should allow the father a chance to know he has a child coming. He'll be interested if he's the man you think he is. You've got to be fair to him."

Tracy saw the pain in her mother's eyes. She watched her dad take out his big white handkerchief and wipe his face.

"Dad. I'll have to give back my scholarship and find a job. I want to try to finish my junior year before the baby comes. With help from you, Mom and Dad, I fully intend to finish all the required courses in biology and try for a teaching certificate, even if it takes me an extra year."

Dad placed his big hands on her shoulders. "You know you'll have our support, honey. We'll welcome a new life into our home."

Mom dried her eyes with the corner of her napkin. "Sweetie, you have our help as long as you need. This is your future and we want to be a part of it."

Next day, Tracy called for appointments with her coach, athletic department, and the dean of admissions. Everything went well, though her coach looked pretty upset until she told him about the baby. She talked with Dr Schuman as a family friend. "Give me a few days, Tracy. The medical community is always looking for bright young people. I'll make a few calls."

A few days later Tracy interviewed with Medi-Serv Associates who hired her part time for the front office in the local surgical center. Tracy continued her exercise regimen without slowing down. She even worked part time. She confessed to her friend Brenda, "I'm enjoying the part time job but I'm also looking forward to a long hot summer without the stress of school. Mom thinks I need to slow down."

She thought about what Mom said. "Tracy! Running three miles a day while six months pregnant can't be good for you or the baby. Check with Dr Schuman and give yourself a break. I'm worried about you."

****

"Oh, Mom, she's so beautiful!" Tracy said. She held her young daughter for the first time.

"Well, she certainly is. She looks just like you. Except the blonde hair and baby blues. Catherine is the second beautiful blonde in our family now."

"You know she does look like Steph, when she was younger, Mom. Look at that little dimple. Her dad has that. I know he'd feel so proud." She broke into tears, a real flooding.

Mom reached for her hand. She leaned down and kissed her forehead.

"Mom, I pray that I've made the right decision, that the three of us will get together. I know it's up to me to make it happen. I believe he's strong enough to forgive me."

Chapter 16

The heat in the Mojave Desert was brutal. Tracy had to stop because Catherine needed lunch, both had to feel hungry. She stopped in the desert town of Baker where the world's tallest thermometer registered 109 degrees. *Thank God for the Mad Greek restaurant, an oasis for tired travelers.*

"I need a break from the drive, honey. Besides it's lunch time, so don't say you're not hungry. I heard your tummy growl."

"Maybe a little. Mom, will it be this hot at Gramma's house? I can't wait to get in the pool. Wish we didn't get hungry so we would get there sooner."

"You know it's always hot at Gramma's house. Put your flip flops on before getting out of the car, sweetie, so the cement won't burn your feet. All your old friends will be there to celebrate your birthday. They missed you when you moved away."

Catherine ran up to her mother, slinging water off her hands. "Mom, Polly said if you pee in the pool, it'll make your hair turn green, forever and ever. Is that right?"

Tracy laughed and looked over at Gramma Mickey. She had her hands in the air. "I'm not sure, honey. But I wouldn't like to see all you girls with bright green hair."

Gramma Mickey said, "It's time for you and your friends to get out of the pool for a while. Ice cream and birthday cake's ready for you under the umbrella. Come on out before the ice cream melts."

Eight screaming kids rushed past the patio where Tracy relaxed with Stephanie, their friends, and mom and dad.

"So, Tracy. You do like living in Los Angeles?" Stephanie said.

"Takes some adjusting. The traffic's bad, but not much worse than here in Las Vegas. The rush just lasts a lot longer."

"Was it hard to find a decent apartment, in a nice area?"

"We've been fortunate so far. A friend at school put us in touch with the owner of a nice condo in Tarzana. We love it. It's gated, has a great pool and the owners nice. Also, Steph, we don't have so many of those days where the temperature gets over a hundred and stays there."

"Sounds really great. How far are you from the beach?"

"About ten miles from Malibu. However, I've found a favorite beach area a little farther north, Paradise Cove. Cat loves it there. We try to make it for a few hours every weekend. It's still in Malibu, but much less congested."

Stephanie took a pull on her pink lemonade. "My friend Valerie teaches at Santa Barbara City College. She's invited me to visit during our Thanksgiving break. Wants a partner for some beach volleyball and hopes I might fall in love with the area as she did."

Mom laughed. "You know darn well that you'll love Santa Barbara. That's where you became addicted to volleyball in the first place. That week we spent at the small beachside motel cost us a fortune."

"My social life drags right now. I need a break. I'm especially looking forward to seeing Valerie."

Tracy raised her glass. "Steph, you make great lemonade." *She really has no idea of a boring social life.*

Mom looked right at Stephanie. "I know you and Valerie both played volleyball in school. I do believe that was the beginning of your real dedication to the game. But why do I sense there may be more to this visit than you're expressing?"

"Oh, Mom, you're right. I may investigate teaching in the public schools there in Santa Barbara. I only avoided mentioning it because you miss Tracy and Catherine so much. Forgive me?"

"Of course, it's time for you to spread your wings and test yourself anyway. Your father and I don't expect either of you to miss out on life's opportunities just because we love you."

Tracy said, "That's wonderful, Stef. Santa Barbara is only a couple of hours drive for us. We'd love that. Cat will be thrilled."

"Don't mention it yet, Tracy. I need a job first. That might not be so easy in Santa Barbara."

After all the kids left, Catherine sipped ice cold lemonade, and talked with Gramma Mickey. She changed the subject.

"Mom said my daddy lives in Los Angeles, Gramma. Do you know him? His name is Mike McGowin, like my name. She said we would look for him in L A."

Mickey looked at Tracy, then back at Catherine. "I've never met your father, honey. But I understand he's a very nice man. I'm sure he'll find you soon, with your mom's help."

Oh my God, don't bring that up right now.

"Do you think he'll like me, Gramma?"

"Oh yes. He'll fall in love with you the first time he sees you, honey. If he knew where you lived, he'd come, see you all the time."

"I'm sorry, sweetie," Tracy said. "I'm sure we'll find him before very long.

Chapter 17

Joel thumbed through the boat's logbook. He found what he was looking for and marked it with a stickie note. They talked about the money. Tracy attempted to draw information from Joel about Mike's job, his family, and anything else she could get. Joel spoke well of Mike and the close family corporation up to a point, then deferred to Mike for answers. After a while he decided to share Mike's log entry with her. She saw him open the book at a marked point.

"I'm going to read Mike's log entry to you," Joel said. "It's entered on the date of departure from Cabo San Lucas, June tenth, including a tempered version of the abuse of two women inside the Naked Mermaid. Mike planned to cover this with you himself."

'A desperate request for assistance from the two women followed an encounter near an old van outside the restaurant. The women appeared to be in distress. They asked for help and accepted an offer of sanctuary aboard this vessel at the Hotel Baha Marina."

Farther along in the log, Joel read another entry.

'While cruising near a small debris field off the Isle of Guadalupe, we observed a large white plastic bag floating in the ocean. It was retrieved for proper disposal. It felt unusual. Upon examination, we discovered nine women's purses containing various identification papers of US Citizens.'

Tracy stopped him there. "So that's how we explain it."

Joel said, "If there's an answer to the problem. Mike, the most resourceful person I've ever known, would find it. As far as the money, neither Mike nor I was excited. It would have been plain stupid to leave it behind. Something practical would have to be worked out."

Joel dumped the two heavy canvas bags onto the teakwood dining table and walked away leaving them alone.

Tracy and Stephanie stepped up to look inside. The smaller of the two bags was opened first. Tracy looked at the thick bricks of currency, all packed in tight with the green side up.

"Are we dreaming, Stef? Does this mean we share in all this money? I'm afraid to touch it. I might wake up back in the ocean, struggling to keep my face out of the water."

"This is no dream, Tracy. I've never met a man like Mike. Why didn't you talk about him years ago? You told me about someone but refused to elaborate, even under duress. And you did have plenty of that."

"At that time in my life, Stef, I was prideful and independent, and believed I was self-sufficient. I also knew what I was in for when I allowed myself to fall deeply in love after the best three days of my life. I was so young. Please don't tell Mike anything about my life since then. I promise. I'll tell him everything before this trip is over. He deserves it. I thought until a few days ago I was over the emotions. Even at this minute, after so long, I still want to curl up in his arms and cry my heart out."

Tracy shifted her concentration back to the canvas bags. "Now, let's count the money."

After counting and taking notes for two hours they returned to the bridge.

"Thanks for the explanation, Joel. That was very enlightening. Now. A few winks on the sofa before we go for the bear."

The pillows stored beneath the couch were small but soft and smooth. She looked through the selection of blankets and spread one over Steph who was already curled up asleep.

At eleven p.m. sharp, Tracy was awakened by a touch on her shoulder. "It's time to wake the sleeping giant. Would you like to do the honors?" Joel said.

"Of course, may I take a couple of private minutes first?"

"Sure, you might also see what's available for a midnight snack. Otherwise, he'll stick with a coffee diet all night."

Tracy tapped on Suite D. She left the door open for light and gazed down at the sleeping man. She had been fascinated by Mike's large masculine look. She recalled again how she moved her fingers over the wide-set eyes and full lips, the passion that consumed her at the time. *I need to get hold of myself.*

She reached out, placed a hand on Mike's forehead. He opened his eyes at once. He looked straight at her, taking a second to focus, then reached up to pull her down on top of himself. She placed her lips on his. She became aware of the sensual contact between their close warm bodies. She didn't resist.

She whispered into his ear, "Please, Mike. We must take a little more time to talk. I'm not concerned about you. It's my own secrets that I fear. I can't have you end up hating me."

Mike removed his hands from Tracy's bottom and helped her stand. "Tracy. I know we have some serious problems to work out. I want you to answer one question first. Are you going to attempt to leave my life again?"

"No, Mike. Only if you decide that would be best."

"Would you care to clarify that for me?"

"Not yet. A girl has to keep a few secrets, you know."

"Okay. Give me a few minutes to brush my teeth and tend to business here and I'll meet you topside. One more thing, Tracy. I believe you knew that I loved you when we kissed goodbye two days before that Christmas. And I still do."

"Yes, I felt that you did. We were both afraid of commitments. I felt that my life was just beginning after I met you."

Mike freshened himself up and joined Joel on the bridge. "How're things in our house of 'what next?' tonight, Joel?"

"So far, things couldn't be better. All systems check out well. I started the water maker for a while. We should run it the rest of the night and tomorrow. I logged our cruise activity since your latest entry. You seem to have a plan for the girls. Do you think they can pull it off without a problem?"

"Yeah, I do. They're both very bright. We should go over everything with them after breakfast tomorrow morning. Anything new on the weather?"

"Not much has changed. It looks like you were right about slowing down to let that stuff ahead of us settle out some. I backed off to only eight knots. It looks like we can get a full three hundred miles under the bottom before we contend with that pressure gradient. The last hundred miles off Point Loma might be a bit rough."

Mike turned to see Tracy with a tray of sandwiches. "Beware of beautiful angels bearing gifts, Joel. There may be a broken heart hiding behind that smile."

She chuckled at Mike's serious look. "A broken heart means a tender heart. It can be repaired with the help of the right repairman. How's the coffee holding out for the single cup maker?"

Joel said, "Perhaps you could bring out more of the bold roast, Tracy. That seems to go faster."

Mike said, "Tracy, we're missing about a million dollars somewhere. I think I should pat you down. It looks like something's hidden in your bra."

Tracy laughed. "By the time you finished checking out my bra, big boy, you wouldn't remember what you were looking for." She passed Joel a steaming coffee.

He laughed so hard he spilled coffee down the back of Mike's leg.

"That serves him right, Joel. Thanks. Is it okay to take Mike below to check his injury and change the bandage? It won't take long, perhaps long enough time to beat him with a stick and clean up his injury."

Tracy located the medical kit and placed several cotton pads next to the bottle of alcohol she used for cleaning and disinfecting the wound. She, turned to Mike. He'd been trying to deal with unwanted sexual stimulation.

"I'm sorry, Tracy. This wouldn't be a problem with anyone but you. I'm feeling too emotional at the moment."

"I understand, Mike. I'm also pleased to hear that. Would you like me to leave?"

"No! Just go ahead with the doctoring. Let's get this over with." He reached for a pillow and held it close while Tracy pulled his fishing shorts down below his butt.

"Mike! This thing's not closing like it should. It doesn't seem to be infected. Maybe the antibiotic has controlled the infection. You'll have a very large scar, no doubt."

"That's good, Tracy. Someday as an old man. I can show it to our grandchildren and brag about how it all happened."

Tracy turned away for a moment. She wiped her eyes, with a tissue, washed her hands again and returned to place a lengthy section of gauze over the wound.

Joel stopped in the salon to finish off a thick ham and cheese sandwich before retiring. "Did you tell Mike about the tally that you and Stephanie arrived at last evening?"

"No, I want Mike to ask about it. What's wrong with that guy?"

"You know him, Tracy. That's not what's on his mind since you arrived. He's never been so gentle with anyone. I'm glad to see the interest, for both of you."

Chapter 18

Mike dialed the number in Washington. He knew the satellite telephone wouldn't identify the caller. He grinned to himself in spite of the seriousness of the call. After five or six long rings, he was certain a machine wouldn't be taking the call. He grinned again.

"This had better be good, whoever the hell you are!" said the strong, somewhat groggy voice.

"Don't badger me about disrupting your beauty sleep. Take your hand off your girlfriend's tush, Max. I know it's late and the dream's hot, but this can't wait

"Damn you, McGowin. If I'd known it was you, I would've turned off the damn phone. Are you under arrest for pissing in public? Just pay the fine, serve the ten days. I'm going back to sleep."

Mike laughed again. "In all seriousness, Max. This is important. I wouldn't be calling you at this hour otherwise. I can't discuss the matter in detail over the air. It's important enough that I'm asking you to fly to California immediately for a confidential meeting with me. I'm calling from a private vessel in Mexican waters.

I'll be checking in with customs on the morning of the nineteenth in San Diego."

"That's ridiculous, Mike. Are you serious about this? You're talking about today. It's already three a.m. on the nineteenth here. I don't believe you'd waste my time, but I need some help here. Give me what you can in a safe manner. I'll attempt to decide. It may not be possible to get there as quick as you want."

"This is what I can give you now. Onboard with me are potential witnesses to serious crimes. Quite possibly, multiple killings. It could be big, Max. Their lives are in danger. They can't leave this vessel in safety. Let me stress this: you'll not be disappointed at the results of this meeting. You have access to an agency jet. Its use will be justified after you meet me at customs and come aboard to interview the witnesses. You may decide how to proceed from that point."

"All right, let me see what can be done in this short time frame. Give me the number of that satellite phone. It's available twenty-four seven?"

"Yes, for sure. Thanks, old friend. I look forward to seeing you in a few hours." Mike massaged his temples with his thumbs for a few seconds before reaching for the log-book. *Max is a detail man. I have to provide all pertinent information, making it concise. He's not always sweetness and light.* He poured himself another cup of black coffee. He thought more about Max's position now, as deputy director. He thought back to their last deployment together. *A damn fine leader, suffered terribly.*

Mike turned off all lighting, including instrumentation. He left only light from the radar providing light on the bridge. He relaxed in the comfortable command chair and looked out at the smooth moonlit ocean, allowing his mind to review the situation ahead. An hour later, he walked out on deck. He let the fresh sea breeze stimulate his energy level, then returned to the control station.

Mike remembered long talks with Max and the many stressful decisions made together under difficult circumstances. A man of principle, he would trust his friend. He watched the moon disappear behind low hanging clouds, feeling the stress fall away. For the first time he felt more certain of a favorable outcome to their problem.

Chapter 19

August Palmyra and Mark Wynn landed at a small airport near Todos-Santos, Mexico for lunch and refueling of the Piper Seneca. Augustine called Howell to report in as ordered.

"No luck, Lance. We flew over the Los Coronado Islands. Like everywhere else we've been, there's nothing at all resembling your big boat. We've searched the vicinity of the Coronados and nearby mainland extremely well. I suggest we end it here."

"The hell you say. That won't fly."

"Yes, we've checked all the harbors on both sides of the Baha Peninsula. I'll bet money those damn guys crossed into the US and continued north toward Canada. The caper must've started right after that first meeting with shipping agents on June sixteenth."

"Okay, August. We'd better forget about that for the time being, but it's not over. Come in as fast as you can get here. We're running behind in prepping the shipment. I need you here to make it happen."

"I can be in San Quentin by four this afternoon. Soon enough?"

"Yea, tell Mark Wynn to be ready for more work when we get this shipment outta here. Find out if he can get clearance into the US. We're not finished with the Guerrero situation."

Howell sat in the pilot house talking with Captain Attilio Mendez. The captain had rushed into port after a call from Howell. The captain's seventy-foot trawler normally moored at one of the private docks controlled by Lance.

"You understand, Captain. All four trawlers are to be loaded and ready by six tomorrow evening. As usual each trawler must carry two pangas on deck, ready, but empty of cargo in case snoopers are checking you out from the air. The entire load of product must be held below until you rendezvous with the freighter. You also have thirteen paying passengers to be delivered ashore between San Diego and Point Conception. It's up to you to determine how they are assigned space in the pangas with the product. Pass this on to the operators."

"I understand, Lance. Me and Augustine always figure out those things while product's being loaded onboard the mothership. So, you and Augustine will make the trip aboard my vessel?"

"Yes. I'm sure you're aware of my missing yacht and the effort we're making to track down the Guerreros."

"I know those two, Lance. Somehow this doesn't seem like their kind of planning. Someone else must be a part of it. Have you considered all of your key people here and in the States?"

"I've looked at all our people. None are missing and none seem capable of pulling it off on such short notice. How about some of those trawler owners we've worked with in the past? Do you have any ideas about that?"

"No, I can't think of anyone that crazy, Lance. Are you boarding tomorrow evening?"

"Yes. Augustine may check in with you tonight. I'll be here until the product is packaged and loaded tomorrow. I have the usual meeting with the ship owner's agent at the rendezvous point. Can you accommodate everyone with margaritas in your pilot house?"

"Sure. I look forward to finding out what those shippers know, if anything, about that last meeting with the brothers who stole your boat. I know most of those guys."

Augustine entered Lance's office. He waited for Lance to hang up the phone. "I have one bit of good news, Lance. The private investigator we hired to locate the bastard who attacked you in Cabo just called in with his report. He believes the son of a bitch was from a private yacht passing through Cabo, heading back to California. You want this information now or after this delivery's taken care of?"

"I don't joke about this, August. Give me what you have!"

"The detective is Pedro Medina. He located a taxi driver that picked up two men near the restaurant where you were attacked. He delivered them to a small restaurant across town. He followed up from there. The two fit your description of the men you want. One was big and muscular. They came ashore from a private yacht moored at the Baha Hotel Marina overnight. The boat departed for California before daylight the morning after the attack. The yacht is documented to the McGowin Trust in Los Angeles, whatever that is. Would you like him to go on to LA and attempt to locate those men?"

"Is this another shot in the dark? Or do you feel comfortable with the information?"

"I would say it's as good as you're going to get, Lance. But is it worth the expense? After all, locating your own yacht at least offers the possibility of some return on your investment."

"To hell with the investment, August! This is personal. Have Pedro go ahead and follow up now. I want that information in my hands by the time we return from the rendezvous."

In an up-beat mood, Howell had Augustine Palmyra and Attilio Mendez meet him in the warehouse where men packed the shipment for loading onto trawlers. He answered his phone and moved away for greater privacy.

He returned to the others after several minutes on the phone in a different mood.

"Some serious shit must be happening. I may have a problem in Mexico. That was the big honcho. All shipments and activity in our operating areas are to be stopped at once. Contacts with Mexican law enforcement advised that American drug people are snooping around inside Mexico. We'd better stand down until our people locate the problem and take care of it. The mothership operation is halted until further notice."

"Listen to me, Augustine. This could be the break we need to locate that bastard. The jefe says we may be closed down for weeks. I want you to lock up this place tight. Put extra security around the compound, twenty-four-seven. I don't like the coincidence of this and our missing boat. Have either of you picked up anything at all? Those guys may have taken the money, gone north and sold out."

Augustine shook his head. "Lance, I doubt that. They're afraid of any American law enforcement. They could be hiding out here in Mexico where they have a lot of family."

"I hope you're right, August. They'd be charged with murder in a New York minute." He became quiet. *Can't share info with associates.* Too much of his personal funds were hidden aboard the yacht.

"Get that guy, Mark Wynn, on the phone and see if he can get clearance into California. I'm going to my place in Long Beach to figure things out. As soon as Pedro gets what we need, you come on up. We have a lot to do while waiting for our people to figure out what's happening down here. Our primary objective now should be getting answers. We can do that just as well from Long Beach, and I can concentrate on getting that bastard that attacked me in Cabo."

Lance called a meeting at his fifth-floor condominium overlooking Long Beach Harbor. He sat with Augustine and Pedro Medina, their investigator.

He wanted that report. "Yes, Mr Howell, the man's name is Mike McGowin. He's a member of a wealthy, well known family in the Los Angeles business community. He's very active in the family corporation with offices on Santa Monica Boulevard in West Los Angeles."

Augustine said, "Chief! You may have this tiger by the tail, but something tells me it's time to turn him loose. Even if he's your man this thing has an enormous downside. This tiger may have sharp teeth."

"You don't get it, Augustine. The bastard humiliated me in my own hometown. No one has ever done that and lived. Your job now is to put three of the biggest and meanest bastards in our organization to work with me when we confront this asshole. This is too big for big Jake to handle alone. Of course, we'll choose the time and the place to make things happen."

Lance squinted at Medina. "Pedro, can you find this man and tail him for me?"

"Oh yes. He's away on his boat. His father has a favorite place at Catalina Island. I'll locate the boat. He'll be there. How soon do you need this?"

"I want the information now. If he's there on the boat, that fits in perfect with my plans. You get this fact confirmed and in my hands by tomorrow afternoon, you'll earn a nice bonus. You have a description and the name of the boat, I presume?"

"Yes, sir, I'll do a sightseeing tour by air and locate his boat that way. If we find it fast, I can be put on the ground to make sure he's onboard. It'll be faster if I call you with this information. Is that all right?"

At four in the morning, Lance attempted to ignore the ringing telephone. The damn thing kept ringing. Half asleep, he finally picked up the phone, irritated. "Oh! I'm sorry boss. It's been a short night." For the next twenty minutes his only comment was, "Yes, I understand. Yes, I'll handle the problem."

Lance felt the pressure. He organized his thoughts and called Augustine Palmira in for a meeting at a small waterfront restaurant in Long Beach Harbor. "Plans have changed, August. You have to return to San Quentin now and get product ready. We have a new schedule coming tomorrow. They're blaming me for the delay, and it's all because of those two women in Cabo. The family filed a missing person report and sent agents into Mexico to investigate their disappearance. They were asking questions around Cabo and seemed to know that the girls had been seen in that restaurant. My only choice now is to stay here and finish off the bastard that identified the women from family photographs. Pedro Medina's report placed the big yacht at Two Harbors, Catalina Island. If the men you have coming are good, this problem should be over within twenty-four hours, then I can get back to more productive work."

Within hours he had three men from his Southern California distribution network in front of him. "You men understand just what we have to do and can handle it, right? The five thousand I'm paying for this job may seem like easy money. Let me tell you, this man and his partner won't go down easy. I want him beat nearly to death but kept alive so he can see me put the knife to his throat and push it into his brain stem."

He looked at Big Jake. "We made arrangements with a local fisherman to carry the four of us to the area where his boat's moored. We'll anchor as close to his boat as possible. The local will use his rubber dingy to move around, looking the situation over until midnight. Then he'll return with a full report of everything that's happening onboard. After that, it's our problem to solve. We'll use the rubber dingy to move around until we feel the time is right to strike. We go aboard and make things happen. There's no reason for those two men to expect trouble in that peaceful harbor."

Big Jake Hayward, at six feet six inches tall, weighed in at three hundred pounds. He smirked and spoke up to his long-time boss. "Hell, Lance, I think you should call off this extra help here and let me do the job just like we've always done. We've taken care of much bigger problems without any trouble."

"Hell no, Jake. This is critically important to me. You may be full of undiluted meanness, but this is personal. I want it finished while we have him in the cross hairs. You might as well know that I'm in trouble with the top people in Mexico because this bastard stuck his big nose into my business. I can't have that happen. I want his ass now."

He studied the scarred face of Big Jake. "You're the best man for the job, Jake, but you're also known as an associate of mine with an outstanding warrant and long arrest record, so don't get picked up. You shouldn't even be here. You can see why this is important to me. I want this thing finished now. You have plenty of backup, so use it. I can't afford a screw up."

Soon after midnight, Captain Shorty Munoz returned with his report. "Two men sat in the cockpit drinking beer until around eleven before going down. They turned the lights out in two separate rooms in the aft section of the yacht. There was nothing at all happening for the hour following lights out. One man was large and muscular and the other was medium height and slim."

Three big men stepped into a small rubber dingy and started up the outboard motor.

Chapter 20

Tracy raised her head to see what caused a shadow over her book. She pointed at a young seagull hovering overhead hoping for a morsel of food.

Mike was more fascinated with the breeze playing tricks with Tracy's hair. He resisted a desire to lean over and nibble her ear. "I'm glad we have time to talk," he said. "You know we still have a lot to deal with before any of us feel comfortable with this situation. First, we must deal with the authorities in San Diego."

"I know, Mike. I'm sorry for all the trouble. You've been wonderful to Stephanie and me."

"You and Stephanie won't be safe until everything's handled the right way. Before we get into how much money's involved here, how we need to handle everything, we have a responsibility to those poor women who met up with this guy, Howell. If we handle that part of the situation, maybe the money part will work itself out. Have you thought about what would happen if anyone tried to deposit large sums of money like we're dealing with, into a personal bank account?"

"I've thought about all of this, Mike. I felt all along you'd work it out. God knows, Stephanie and I could use a windfall. But we'll be all right without all that money. She's not destitute, neither am I."

"So, look. Our primary consideration must be for those women whose purses we found. We have-to be sure they're still missing. Here's the dilemma. First, we need to lie to the customs authorities in San Diego. I wish there could be another way.

He thought hard for a moment. "You and Stephanie gotta get your stories straight. Back up our log entry about meeting you outside the restaurant where you had that bad experience with Lance. After your fight in the ladies' room, you ran outside where you caught us on our way out. That's where you agreed to come with Joel and me back to the yacht moored at the Hotel Baha Marina. You both had your purses with you. That's going to be the most difficult part for you to deal with. Finding yours along with all the others would be too much of a coincidence. Remember, we had a short cab ride. A couple of miles to the marina. Say nothing about being held on Lance's boat. That'll come out later."

Mike removed his cap and ruffled his hair back. "The rest of your story should be just the way it happened. You should go over the entire story, so you both to tell the same thing. Go over it with Stephanie so it all sounds natural."

Mike pulled on his beer. "That's not going to be all. You may have to provide the real story to the FBI later.

The real story at customs would get us arrested, then months of investigations, possibly involving Mexico. I don't want you thinking about that now. I plan on getting the FBI involved with the real story after we're through customs in San Diego. Do you feel confident you and Stephanie can handle your end of all this?"

"Of course we can, Mike. I'm glad we'll get the real story out later though. Do you think the FBI will be able to get Lance Howell?"

"I'm pretty sure, Tracy. We've got hard evidence as well as your and Stephanie's testimony."

Tracy left the deck chair. She leaned over to kiss Mike, then, sat down on his knee. She stayed there.

He felt a closeness. He sensed her desire to belong.

Mike pulled her on into his lap, then tight against his body. He felt her breath against his hair. He smelled her body, the soap from her shower. They remained that way for a long while.

Mike relieved Joel on the bridge. Each placed a series of business-related telephone calls to the LA office and work sites. Each man utilized a full hour on the phone, followed by a half hour of serious discussion.

Tracy poured two cups of coffee. She handed one to Mike. "Would you like a sandwich with the coffee?"

"Thanks, the coffee's fine for now. Do you feel like telling me how much money we have to deal with from those two bags?"

"I thought you'd never ask. The one and only written list, the one you wanted, we tucked away with your things in the top drawer near your bed. The grand total is an unimagined $1,750,000 between the two bags. Now tell me the truth. What can we expect from this mess? Will we be able to share in all that money?"

"I can't promise anything. If they release some of it, that should go to you, Stephanie and Joel."

"Oh, Mike, I can't believe it. I've never ever expected to have more than a barely comfortable living."

"Remember. There are no guarantees at this point. we'll have to see how it plays out. Listen to me, Tracy. That money won't be as important to you now. You've had a terrible time of it. You could be dead. You deserve what you end up with. Now! Would you mind telling me what's been going on in your life? Your personal life?"

Chapter 21

"Mike, I want you to know. I've kept a terrible secret from you. I've waited, even prayed for an opportunity to ask your forgiveness. There's something that may cause you pain. I claim my own cowardice. My desire to not interfere with your goals, your plans with the Army. The career you talked about. I was wrong not answering you after we said goodbye so long ago." She held her breath. She'd been unusually quiet for the last hour, while asking God for his help.

He looked into her eyes, with obvious interest.

She tried to still her nervous hands. She took both his hands in hers. "Mike, you have a beautiful ten-year-old, blonde, blue-eyed daughter, bearing the name of a father she's never known. Please forgive me."

Tracy heard Mike catch his breath. He stared at her.

He dropped her hands, grabbing her shoulders. He kept on staring into her eyes. "What the hell's going on here, Tracy? Are you sure about what you're saying?"

"Forgive me, please. I beg of you, Mike. I've deprived you of the most cherished blessing life can give us. She felt her heart pound. *Please God, let him understand.* "Yes Mike. I named her Catherine. Catherine McGowin. She's your daughter, Mike. I always planned to share this beautiful, lovable and very bright daughter of ours, but couldn't find the courage to face you. I moved to California to live, to hopefully run into you some day."

His eyes shone with dampness. "Damn you, Tracy. How in hell could you do something like this? We cared for each other!" He turned away. "Did you hate me that much?"

She tried not to break but her tears betrayed her. Would he understand? *Please God let him understand.* "After a time, I convinced myself that you'd moved on with your life, most likely with a loving wife and children. I dreaded you'd hate me, for not sharing our wonderful child. I soon realized my terrible deception. My dream of us together, recapturing what we both felt after that short time we had together. I became frightened it would never happen."

Mike continued to stare at her. He took in every word. *What is he thinking?* She watched him step to the helm, look at the radar, gaze out at the dark sea. He came back to her.

"Tell me about her, Tracy. When was she born? Why would you do such a thing? We loved each other. What does she look like? Show me something, a picture. Anything to ease my mind. That's not like you, the girl I knew. The one I fell in love with."

"I have a picture in my purse, Mike. You'll see for yourself."

"Why didn't you tell me all this? I had a right to know."

"Catherine longs to know her father. I can't wait till you and Catherine meet. You will love each other so much it makes my heart ache."

Tracy returned with a picture. "Look, Mike. The dimple, know anyone with a little family trait like that?"

He smiled for the first time. "My mother, Tracy. She looks just like my mother, when she was young. Even as an adult, beautiful."

"You, Mike! Your own little dimple on your left cheek. You know it, don't you?"

"She asks about her father?"

"All the time, Mike. She's full of questions. She knows as much about you as I do. She sees you through my eyes."

"It must have been hard for you, all alone, losing your scholarship. I only wish you'd shared with me. That's what love's all about. Sharing everything. I thought I knew you, respected your integrity."

"Mike. If you forgive me, can't we start over, a happy family together?"

"I don't know, Tracy. I feel betrayed."

Chapter 22

Blue Dolphin rose high on a large swell and dropped into the trough. Mike studied the horizon. Strong winds blew the tops off waves. It didn't look good. *Bad weather on into San Diego. Damn weather system should have moved on by now.* He drank coffee from a thermos cup, studied the wind direction again. A slight change, more from the west, rough. *Been blessed with great sea conditions over last three hundred miles.*

Tracy got off the couch and staggered her way over to Mike. She gripped his arm.

"Better get ready for more rough conditions ahead," he said. "I want you and Steff to take two Dramamine tablets now. Grab a barf bag and work your way down to your cabin. There's less motion down there and I won't have to worry about either of you getting hurt. Snuggle up in bed and try to doze off to sleep. But keep the bags handy."

"Seems like a strange storm, only wind and white-caps," she said.

"This's a dry storm sweetheart. We're dealing with counter-clock-wise winds from a low-pressure trough off the California coast, merging with clockwise winds generated by a high stationed over Mexico, commonly known as a pressure gradient. We have to pass through the area between the two systems where the winds hit the greatest velocity."

Mike smiled at Tracy, then reached down to cover her hand with his. "We're going to be very busy on the bridge through this thing, honey. I'll worry a lot less knowing you and Stephanie are safe in your bunks. We could enter a worse mess by midnight."

He saw Joel come back. "Hey, Joel, we bought ourselves several hundred miles of good weather, but it looks like we're entering the area of disturbance now. Please see that our ladies get tucked away in bed then check the tenders and water toys. Go through the entire vessel, including all galley supplies, lock all refrigerator and freezers. Oh hell, make sure you double check everything before joining me back on the bridge. We have a lot to deal with tonight."

"I'm ahead of you, Mike. We expected this so I started checking things out early. The bilge pumps and fuel filter pressure are good. the engine room can handle anything thrown our way."

"Great, Joel. We're ahead of the game, won't be fighting a heavy downpour. Winds will gust over fifty-miles-per-hour, seas running eight-to-twelve-feet with short intervals." He looked at Tracy. "I'm concerned about the girls."

Tracy grabbed his wrist. She looked reluctant to leave. "Joel asked Steffi and me to go through the boat with him earlier, Mike. We stowed small stuff in drawers and cabinets, got all the towels and deck chairs off the sundeck, checked the doors and lockers."

"Thank you, ladies. Now, let's try to ride this thing out without anyone getting hurt."

Stephanie stood up to leave. "How long do you expect this to last, Mike?"

"Look, we may have to fight this storm all through the night, maybe on into San Diego. To be on the safe side, you guys should go ahead and take the anti-nausea tablets and hunker down until we're out of this mess. Just keep those bags handy.

"Joel! While you're down below, double check the scuba tank storage rack. Wouldn't be happy if one of those things fell off the rack, busted the neck off and shot away like a rocket. Two thousand pounds of compressed air behind it could create a problem."

A strong gust of wind howled through the superstructure above. Wind speed increased. *Not even a barbed-wire fence to slow the velocity off the wide Pacific*, he thought. *High waves, deep troughs will stress the ship and crew.*

Blue Dolphin encountered more pitch and roll. Mike altered course. He turned stern quarter to the violence, ran with the sea. That smoothed out the ride. He held the course for thirty minutes, then changed course again. A west by north heading for thirty minutes. He followed a zig-zag course for two hours, providing more stability. He moved his eyes from compass to radar and back again, with growing concern for a small target showing up from time to time at three miles, about ten degrees off port.

Mike locked down the helm long enough to fine-tune the radar. He got a better picture. *Wouldn't like smacking into one of those big steel containers lost from a ship. They lose them in bad weather sometime. Where's Joel, he should be back by now. Must have a problem down below.* He adjusted course, checked radar again. The unknown object now at quarter mile. He changed course once more, placed object downwind on starboard side. He picked up high resolution glasses.

Joel grabbed onto Mike's chair. "Sorry, Mike. The steel cage door protecting the scuba tanks banged open, a broken latch. Had to round up some repair gear and re-position the tanks. Came close to a disaster. The girls are using the bags. I left some extra with dry towels, and a damp cloth for each."

"Good man. It looks like we have a vessel in distress out there. Look for a weak light blinking off to starboard. Take the helm for a moment, Joel. Keep the object where it is now. I'll take the glasses up front of the helm for a better look."

Saltwater blanked the windows in front. Joel turned on the freshwater wash, allowed the wipers to do a better job.

The situation became clear at once. "I'll be damned, Joel, someone's signaling with a weak flashlight. Slow to minimum headway. Let's figure this thing out. No doubt his radio's down. I got nothing all night on channel sixteen. That looks like a thirty or forty-foot sloop with the mast dragging in the water, people in the cockpit."

"Hope they're all wearing life vests, Mike."

Chapter 23

Mike studied the storm ravaged vessel with his binoculars. "That damn thing's on the verge of sinking! We can't waste time, Joel. The sea's too rough for a vessel-to-vessel rescue. The trough's too deep, the frequency too short. Here's what we need do, the only way. Take control, Joel, now. Keep her downwind of the other boat, with our swim platform about twenty-five feet away from the debris hanging over the side."

"I can manage that, pal. I'll have to use the cockpit controls. What do we do next?"

"I'll pass a long line over to the people in the boat, our end secured here. If I yell out loud, you know the line's in the water, too close to the propellers. Move us forward as slow as you can until I've recovered the slack. Then, get in position again for another throw. We don't have a monkey fist. That would make it too simple."

"Mike! that boat's filling with water, sinking fast. Go with the line over now."

With safety harness in place, Mike held a coiled hundred-foot ski tow rope. He hoped the handle was heavy enough to make the thirty-foot toss. He yelled at Joel, "Get on the hailer. Have them tie one person at a time to the line, loop it through the space at the handle, pull it tight under the arms of the first person to go. I'll pull them over and up."

Joel turned on bright lights in the superstructure. The entire area lit up, showing the vessel filling with water. Mike made his first throw. A tall man grabbed the line and looped it around the nearest woman.

Mike yanked the woman over the side into the water. His safety harness allowed him to put his full strength into the pull. She flailed about, looked terrified. He pulled the woman in close, let out a small amount of line, then allowed the rolling wave behind to dump her at his feet in a foot of swirling water. He removed the line and guided her up into the cockpit.

He rapidly recoiled the line and made a second toss. The same man made another accurate grab. The water-logged vessel rose on a large wave, ripped the line from his hands, throwing him into the boiling sea between the two boats.

Joel powered *Blue Dolphin* farther away when the stricken sailboat rolled down the trough, toward the man in the water. His voice blared. "She's filling with water, Mike. Everyone needs to grab the next toss."

Mike re-coiled the line quickly, tossed it to the two people in the sinking boat. One person in the water, motioned for the others. They grabbed the line and jumped in his direction. All three struggled to hold on.

Mike watched the trio grab each other's lifejacket with one hand. Some held the line tight with the other.

The stern of *Blue Dolphin* rose high on a swell, threatened to come down on top of people in the water.

Joel throttled forward again, briefly.

Mike let out slack as she slid down the trough, then pulled all three people onto the swim platform in a foam-covered mass. He noticed stiffness. Obviously chilled, moving slow, with hyperthermia.

Barely on board, survivors watched their stricken vessel disappear beneath the waves.

Joel saw they were all safely in the cockpit. He eased the *Dolphin* away and turned into the wind to reduce the roll.

"Good job, Joel," Mike said. He helped the shivering refugees into the salon, pleased to see Tracy and Stephanie standing there with large dry towels. "We have to get these folks below and out of the wet clothing. Grab warm blankets. Wrap them up well. I'll meet you in the salon with hot coffee."

George Hampton explained that he and his wife Susan were unfortunate owners of *Southwind*, a fine forty-one-foot sloop. He introduced their fellow survivors, Frank and Doris, their cruise guests for the past month. He expressed his gratitude for responding to their needs in such professional manner. "We lost hope, then, the lights of your vessel appeared,"

Mike said, "George, you are aware I have to report the abandonment and sinking of your vessel. Do you have any objections?"

"No, of course not. Our families will be pleased to hear that we're safe aboard your yacht. Thank you again, Mike."

Mike asked Tracy to take charge of the group. He excused himself to join Joel on the bridge. "I have to call in this incident to the coast guard in San Diego. You did a hell of a job at the controls, Joel. No one could've done as well. If I can't raise the coast guard by sat phone this time of night, I'll go to the emergency radio frequency."

"This is US Coast Guard, San Diego California. How may I help you, sir?"

"Coast Guard, this is the U.S. registered yacht *Blue Dolphin*. Owner, the McGowin Trust of Los Angeles, California. I wish to report a rescue at sea of four persons from a foundering vessel. Can you take the report?"

"Yes, sir, Captain. What is your name please?"

"My name is Mike McGowin, one of the registered owners of this vessel. If you would allow me to provide you with the information I have. Then I'll attempt to answer all further questions. There's no longer a danger or further risk to life. We have taken onboard, the following persons: Mr and Mrs George Hampton of Pacific Palisades, California and Mr and Mrs Frank Morris of Santa Monica, California. I found no obvious injuries that need immediate attention. The vessel was abandoned at longitude 31 minutes, 59 seconds north and latitude 117 minutes, 34 seconds west. Heading from San Diego is 180 degrees, due south, approximately sixty-five nautical miles from San Diego and fifty miles west of El Pescadero, Mexico on a heading of 256 degrees west. We're now underway for San Diego and anticipate arriving coast guard there not earlier than five-fifteen a.m. or later than six-thirty a.m. Pacific time. Yes, in answer to your question, you may reach us at the number given any time between now and our arrival time. Thank you, sir. This is the vessel *Blue Dolphin.* International documentation number confirmed. This call completed."

"Mike, you go down and take care of things below. I can handle it here. We'll run with the swell a short time to reduce roll, returning to our course."

"Okay, Joel. I'll get fresh coffee to you right away. The stabilizers are helping, now that we have good headway, running with the wind."

Stephanie saw Mike on the stairs. "How's Joel?"

"He's tired and stressed, Steffi. He can't get away from the helm long enough to get his coffee. Could you make your way topside with some of those sweet rolls? Use the single cup coffee maker there in the upper salon for his coffee. Hold on tight, okay. We don't want an injury after everything else you've been through."

Mike reached for the coffee offered by Tracy and sat down near George and Lucy Hampton. "I'm sorry for your loss, George. That's got to be tough, losing such a fine vessel."

"Yes, like losing one of the family. Lucy and I've pampered her for twenty-seven years and enjoyed every minute of it. Of course, we're grateful that our friends here, Doris and Frank, survived without serious injury."

"Do you mind telling me about it, George? I'm curious how such a fine vessel can flounder."

"Well, we entered the storm area over twelve hours before losing the mast. The wind grew too strong to keep sufficient sail for adequate headway, so we engaged the auxiliary power. We used a little sail as a steadying factor. We seemed to be weathering well. Around ten at night or shortly thereafter, what I believe to be a huge rogue wave caught us broadside with those strong winds. We rolled far enough into the trough to dip the mast. It held us there, flooded the cockpit, throwing sea water down into the cabin. That's when we lost the radio."

George coughed hard before speaking again. "Within a minute, she tried to right herself. The mast snapped. Then came a cracking and scraping noise that caused me to believe we were losing the keel or the hull was breaking up. The engine continued to run for a few minutes then died. We had lights in the cabin for a bit longer after that. I tried to figure out what to do next. No one panicked, Mike. I could not feel prouder of Frank and Doris. They stood steadfast throughout the entire ordeal."

Mike listened intently. "By the way, George. I'll enter your account of the disaster into our ship's log. That'll remain a permanent record should you require as much for your insurance company. I expect you'll have a long tiring session with the coast guard in San Diego. Let me know if I can be of any help to you."

Mike thought of his own problems to deal with in San Diego. He counted on his old buddy Max getting there to help work out a solution.

Chapter 24

Assistant FBI Director Max Findley presented his credentials to an agent behind the desk. Port of San Diego, huh! *Mike wouldn't bring me out here for a damn boondoggle. This might be interesting.*

"Captain McGowin and his vessel participated in a rescue at sea during the early morning hours, Special Agent Findley. Would your appointment have anything to do with that rescue?"

Not sure, Max hesitated. "I believe our business to be a separate matter. Captain McGowin has a relationship with the Bureau office in Washington. I can wait until his vessel is cleared, if you say so."

"We're familiar with the captain and his vessel. Help yourself to coffee and whatever's left in the lounge. It shouldn't be long, sir."

Max watched agents come and go from a large plate glass window. He wondered what was going on.

The door cracked open. "Captain McGowin has cleared customs, Agent Findley. You may board the vessel."

"Hi, Max. You look like Harvey the six-foot rabbit with those red eyes."

"Don't push your luck, Mr Yachtsman. I could arrest you and bill you for my expenses out here. You'd better have a damn good story."

Mike introduced Joel, Tracy, and Stephanie. "Give us a moment to ourselves, guys." He took Max to the pilot house for privacy. He stepped to the overhead console, checked all the ship's communication systems. He made sure none of their conversation could be overheard.

"So, this is how the privileged few live. How elegant!" He gave Mike a hearty embrace.

"Hell, Max. I chose my old man carefully, so I could enjoy the good life. Good wine, bad women. Better fasten your seat belt, old friend. I'm about to tell you a strange, almost unbelievable story. I'll give you everything and rely on your judgment."

Max expected this to be solid, or he wouldn't be here. "Let me get my recorder set up, Mike."

"The two women you just met were kidnapped, and held on a boat off the coast of Mexico. Joel and I became involved by aiding their escape from members of the Mexican drug cartel holding them captive. We have evidence of more missing American women who have either been sold into the sex trade or murdered."

"I hope you can back up all this. It sounds hot. Was that sailboat crew involved?"

"No, Max. The large plastic trash bag there on the deck holds water-soaked handbags, complete with identification, for nine individual American citizens."

"Hold up a bit, let me see what you have, Mike." He pulled out one of the women's bags, raked through it quickly. Okay, move on, Mike."

"They're all women I believe taken and held the same as Tracy and her sister, Stephanie. The other two canvas bags contain an unbelievable amount of hard U.S. currency, liberated from the Mexican drug cartel that held these women, to be sold as sex slaves. I believe the leader and their kidnapper to be Lance Howell, an American citizen operating with the Mexican cartels and having strong organizational ties on both sides of the border with Mexico." Mike stopped. He drank from a water bottle.

Max said, "I may not arrest you after all. Go on with the story."

"I expect you to understand why I've had to keep this closely held within the confines of this vessel. Both women remain in serious danger from the cartel, Max. This guy, Howell, believes Tracy Conwell's dead in accordance with his instructions."

Max held up his hand. "I have to interrupt with a few questions. What instructions?"

"Howell ordered his henchmen to use her any way they wanted, then sink her body. This is only part of the story, Max, let me finish. He and his associates are scrambling to figure out what happened to the boat carrying the sisters and the cartel funds. They had cash on board for a pay-off to shipping associates who moved their cargo loaded panga boats north. I'm sure you understand why we could not ask assistance from the Mexican authorities."

"Well, Mike, I'll say this for you. It's a hell of a scenario as you describe it. I assume the women can back up everything you say. How involved is the other man?"

"Joel works with me as an associate and personal friend, as much involved as I am. You'll understand when you get their stories."

Max snapped off the recorder. "I think we can delay the personal interviews for the time being. Okay! Let's talk generalities before the interviews. You may be creating a hell of a lot of work for me, Mike. I may never forgive you."

Mike returned the grin. "You've been a good friend. I thought you'd want to share in some of the fun, since you FBI guys lead such boring lives in between the political hoopla around Washington."

"So…! What do you expect to happen to all that cash you 'liberated', as you put it?"

"Well, I'm counting on that big brain of yours to help work something out. I'd call it just compensation for the traumatic experience suffered by the sisters. I'd like to see an equal share for Joel Santiago. He placed his life in jeopardy without question, when faced with the consequence of failure to act."

Max paid close attention to the story. He made a few quick notes on a small pocket pad and turned off the recorder again. *Mike: always responsible, looked after his friends. Got to bring in DEA soon. This situation could be bigger than I thought.*

Mike stood up to face his friend. "Look, Max. I appreciate your quick response as a friend as well as the ultimate professional. For my part, I want those guys caught, justice for the missing women. The cash has to be secondary. We could have avoided telling you about the windfall. No one would be the wiser. There's no record and no outside knowledge of the money. Only Howell knew of the cash that he'd stashed, until we discovered it while searching for evidence of the missing women."

"Let me give some thought to this, Mike. First, of course, I need to interview the other three participants. Then I'll verify a few things through DEA. Looks like you stumbled into something."

"One more thing, Max. You need to know I have to keep the Conwell sisters hidden onboard *Blue Dolphin* while cruising on to Ventura County with a one-night layover at Catalina Island. *Blue Dolphin* will be more difficult to locate if the cartel is looking for vessels returning to San Diego or Los Angeles ports from the area their asset is missing. We'll delay docking at our home port in Mandalay Bay until we have a good handle on this thing. Would it be possible for you to come with us all the way to Channel Islands Harbor in Ventura County?"

"Hold on a minute. That might be a little much."

"You'll have full access to the satellite telephone plus cell phone service, once we reach Catalina Island."

Max thought for a moment. "I have a rental car here, Mike, and my bag is still at the hotel. Stay here a bit longer while I sort out a few things."

"I can arrange for a temporary delay through the Harbor Department. Once you're back onboard, your interviewing can go ahead as planned."

Max returned with a small travel bag. "You should know the news media back there are making a lot out of your rescue of the crew from the disabled sailing vessel. They're going to blow your cover." He looked around at the two women. "That's for sure if their interview of survivors drops names of your present company. You hold tight a little longer. I'm going back in and talk to those survivors."

"I should've thought about that. Thank you, Max."

Max returned forty-five minutes later. "I spoke with the survivors and they'll cooperate. I was also able to convince the Coast Guard and Customs people as well. All parties have agreed to be cautious in any conversation with the news media, or anyone else asking questions."

Mike said, "Let's hope for the best."

"The survivors are discussing their ordeal with a few people in the courtesy lounge, waiting for relatives, Mike. The media people are still getting organized. I don't think it'll develop into a problem."

"Thanks, pal. Let's make a getaway before they start looking in our direction. Glad to have you with us, Max. I'm concerned about the safety of these women."

Chapter 25

Mike increased speed a bit, once out of San Diego Bay. The heavy vessel sliced through the five-foot swell rolling down the gulf of Santa Catalina with ease. "Take the helm, Joel. From here on into Avalon Bay. Increase speed, again, once we're away from the kelp beds. Radar's tuned to a quarter mile, because of all those small fishing boats around the kelp beds." *The fishing must be good this morning. Small fishing boats in the kelp beds not unusual, often like fleas on an old dog's back.* They'd hardly made headway until the ceiling increased while cruising dead slow to avoid ramming one in heavy fog.

"Max will have more questions for me during the interviews. I'll stay close to them through the first go-around."

He seated himself a few feet away from Max. He listened to an explanation of procedure to be followed in interviews with Tracy and Stephanie.

Joel's low voice came out of the speaker above. "We're picking up speed again, Mike. Visibility's improved. That'll smooth out the ride a bit and make it three and a half hours to Avalon Bay."

"Copy that, Joel."

He noticed how quiet the state rooms were with the new pod drive system that eliminated vibration and engine noise throughout the vessel. The powerful engines continued their low hum in the salon where interviews were taking place." *Thank dad for that upgrade,* he thought.

Mike sat through Tracy's interview. He remained with Max to answer a few questions himself. The preliminary session went well. He returned to the bridge, thinking of her straight-forward response to questions.

Tracy sat near Joel deep in conversation. She talked about her interview, knowing Joel would be next.

Mike sat down behind them. He relaxed with his chin on his chest, listening to their quiet conversation. Time passed quickly and he soon realized they were staring at the approach to Avalon Harbor, Catalina Island.

"This place is gorgeous! I've never seen anything like it," Tracy said. She pointed at the gauge registering outside air temperature. "Look. A pleasant seventy-four degrees."

Joel slowed to a stop, waiting for permission to enter the harbor. Avalon Bay was flat and calm.

"Joel. Why would you ever go to Mexico when this island paradise is only a few hours away?"

"Ya know, Tracy. I've often wondered the same thing. Mike's dad started making the voyage to the Sea of Cortez to fish the waters around La Paz and Puerto Vallarta years ago with his fishing buddies"

"Well, thank God you made this trip with Mike, for the sake of our daughter," she said.

Mike continued listening to the easy conversation between Tracy and Joel. Why in the world did I ever fail to persevere in my effort to reach out to her years ago? Because he'd convinced himself she'd found someone else. He never got over the short intense affair.

Joel turned toward Mike. "Avalon Harbor Patrol's moving another vessel from our mooring. It'll be another thirty minutes before we can pick up the wand."

Max came up from below. "Hey. What's going on up here? I've reviewed the first recorded interview. We can hold off for the time being. I thought something interesting might be happening, didn't want to miss anything."

The radio blared. "*Blue Dolphin*! Avalon Harbor Patrol. Your mooring's now available. We'll stand by for assistance should you require any."

"Thank you, Harbor Patrol. We'll move into the harbor and pick up our mooring lines now," Joel said.

"Mike, take her in while I grab the wand. I can work the spring line back to the rear tie down alone."

Mike maneuvered the big vessel into the harbor. He eased down the narrow fairway, turned into an even more narrow space between the bow of boats on one side and stern of boats on the other. *Blue Dolphin* spun on its own axis and nosed up to a tall wand standing up near a floating buoy. He watched Joel reach down with a gloved hand, pull up the wand attached to a heavy looped mooring line. He dropped the loop over a stout mooring post, then followed a thin strong spring line to a looped line for the stern cleat.

The radio on the bridge blared again. "*Blue Dolphin*. You appear to be secure. Have a nice stay."

"Max, you're good on the interviews for today?"

"For now, perhaps. Tomorrow, we go over each interview again before transmitting the recordings to Washington with my report. It's very important to check everything for consistency before sending it off. I want all of your candid comments during the review.

"A point of interest to all of you. Checking the identification on each of those women whose handbags you turned in: families have reported all of them missing within the past three years. Furthermore, that man, Howell, has been under suspicion from drug enforcement for more than five years. That lends greater credibility to your stories and the evidence regarding those missing women."

Mike nodded. "That confirms my suspicions, Max. It doesn't make me feel much better about the fate of those women though."

"Now, I understand you serve cocktails aboard this fancy hotel?" Max said.

"Do we ever! The sun's beneath the yardarm somewhere in the world, Max. Then I presume interviews are done for the day."

Tracy jumped to her feet, pointing. "Look, over there. Did you see that? The tall guy in the water, near the dock. He stood up in the bow of the dingy to step onto the dock. A swell lifted the boat away and he tumbled right into the water. His fancy captain's hat floated off out of reach. Why are all those people laughing?"

Joel laughed. "He was showing off in front of the girls in that little boat nearby. Now his fancy yachting outfit's too soggy to visit a nice restaurant."

Max laughed. "Look around at all these fortunate people eating and drinking on their yacht. I wonder what the poor people are doing today?"

Stephanie slapped him lightly on his hand. "There may soon be a few less of us for you to worry about, Agent Findley. If you're as bright as Mike believes." She squeezed his forearm. "Thanks for your help and understanding of our situation."

"Hey, Mike," Tracy said. "Let's get the bar going. You make 'em, I'll pass 'em out. Everyone get settled outside on the sundeck."

Later, Mike cornered Tracy below. "It's nice having a few minutes alone with you. How do you like Max?"

"He certainly asks a lot of detailed questions. Some I had no answers for. He's very nice otherwise, Mike."

"He's like family, Tracy. We can count on his help. Have you been in touch with your folks today… and our daughter?"

"You know darn well I call or text every day, if possible. I should have kept you informed."

"We've been busy, I know. Far too busy for time to share personal information. It's important we fill in the gap between our lives. I want every detail about your life, Tracy. All that I've missed about you and Catherine. My daughter has grown up without me. You have to make time for that soon."

"I know, Mike. I'm anxious to share everything. I want us to know ourselves together, as a family. A family who loves each other. Let's start with a call to Mom and Dad."

He held her gaze without answering.

"Mom and Dad were worried sick during the long period those awful men held us on that boat. Thank God Joel helped us make a call after we found Stephanie. They didn't know what to do. Would it be all right if I tell them about you coming into our lives? Maybe we can both talk to Catherine tomorrow?"

He shook his head. "Tracy. You must remember that you and Steffi are in hiding. Your life depends on everything remaining that way until the FBI and the other agencies close the investigation of your kidnapping. They're gathering information about the smuggling organization." He felt he needed to explain his concern, their waiting for answers from Max's wide range of contacts in DEA.

"Let me suggest this, honey. To start with, tell your parents you and I are together. You can give them all the details later. Let me explain the necessity of secrecy to them. If all goes well tonight, we can talk to Catherine tomorrow. Go ahead, take the drinks outside. Explain that we're making a phone call before leaving for dinner. We'll talk to your parents briefly, then follow up tomorrow."

Tracy nervously made the call. "Hi, Mom. Yes, everything's good. Stephanie's here. I have someone else with me, Mom. Let me talk for a moment. Then I'll put him on. He'd like to talk with you and Dad. It's very important, please listen. I'm with Mike McGowin, Mom. Yes, he needs to explain something, then we'll talk more tomorrow. Yes, Mom. Things couldn't be better. Is Dad available to get on the phone with you? Okay, Mike will speak with you and we'll talk with you both again tomorrow. Here's Mike."

"Hello, Mrs Conwell! Yes. I believe I'm Catherine's father. I'm about ten years late with an introduction. May I call you Mickey? Thank you, Mickey. We're with the FBI for a while. We have limited time to explain. Both of your daughters are safe but I have to stress how important it is they remain in hiding until the FBI can arrest those responsible for holding them prisoner. The bad guys may phone you attempting to get information on the girls' whereabouts. Tell anyone you believe to be strange or suspicious that both your daughters are in Mexico. Express concern that you've not heard from them since June tenth. And stress this point with your husband. That pertains to anyone who may inquire about either of the girls. The people we're dealing with are very smart and we can't take chances."

Mickey said, "Thank you for that information. Would you like to talk with your lovely daughter? She's anxious to know you."

"Thank you, Mickey. You can tell Catherine that she has a father who loves her. He can't wait to see her and hold her in his arms now that he's found her. You can expect a call some time tomorrow from all of us. Tracy, Stephanie and me too."

Tracy pulled Mike's head down and kissed him tenderly. "I'm so happy, Mike. You must think I'm foolish after hiding both Catherine and me from you all those years."

Stephanie rushed in to see Mike and Tracy. "What did Mom and Dad say about Mike? Were they surprised?"

"More than surprised, Stef. Mom was shocked, after I insisted she talk with Mike. I know she and Dad will love him. Dad was out but they're anxious to talk to us tomorrow."

Stephanie grabbed Mike. "I hope you like our family. We're all a little bit nuts most of the time. That's why we need you to keep us out of trouble. I'm so happy for Catherine. Now she has a good daddy to look after her."

Mike woke early. He slipped out of the stateroom he shared with Joel without disturbing him.

He brushed his teeth, took a quick shower and entered the galley. He made two full pots of coffee, poured both into a large vacuum-type decanter. Then he selected a variety of sweets from the pastry case, placed everything on a large butler's tray with paper napkins and plastic plates. He carried it all to the upper salon deck, set out the drop-leaf table and went down to where Tracy was sleeping.

He kissed her softly on the lips, to wake her, trying not to disturb Stephanie. She opened her eyes, encircled his neck with one arm holding him close for a moment before easing out of bed.

Mike looked at food he'd brought up. "I must be crazy putting all this stuff out. You know, of course, we're having a big brunch over the water at the Busy Bee restaurant?"

Tracy slipped in close. "Yes, but it isn't even seven o'clock in the morning. The rooster hasn't crowed yet. I think you're just hungry, lover boy. Maybe you didn't sleep any better than I did. I'm so excited, Mike. I can't wait for your conversation with Catherine. Bet she didn't sleep a wink either last night."

He said, "First of all, I didn't sleep. Second. I'm starved and third. I want to tell you I love you and I'm completely overwhelmed by everything."

Grinning, Mike sat down. He pulled Tracy onto his lap. "I'm still mad at you so get rid of that happy face."

She reached up, pulled his head around and kissed him furiously. They continued to hold each other close.

"I'm glad you rousted me out early," she said. "We need this quiet time together before anyone else interferes. I'd like to stay here on your lap a while longer, maybe forever."

"I'd love that. You're back in my life forever, sweetheart. Until death do us part." He brushed his lips across hers, followed with a light kiss to the tip of her nose. "I never stopped missing you, never even dreamed we had a beautiful daughter. Now, I'm looking forward to a new beginning for the rest of our lives."

She wiped her eyes with a tissue before looking at him. "I know. I've never been more certain of anything in my life. Catherine will love you the way I do. She's dreamed of her father the way I dreamed because I talked about you, described you almost as you are today. You're not much different from the man I fell in love with, maybe a little harder to resist."

Chapter 26

Max centered his thoughts on boats in the anchorage, particularly those anchored near the breakwater. His well-honed instincts and the flood of information from his contacts had set off alarm bells. He connected his phone to the charger and made his decision out of an abundance of caution. He then joined the others having morning coffee on the sun deck.

Stephanie reached out with a tray filled with goodies, a mug of black coffee, and a small plate with bagel and cream cheese.

"Thanks, Stephanie. It sure looks good."

He caught everyone looking at him. "Since we're all together here… We have to change our plans for today in light of how fast drug enforcement jumped on the information provided by you lucky ladies. I had a long night on the telephone with powers that be. Things are coming together fast, much faster than expected."

He focused on Mike. "You've been identified by Howell and his crowd. They're out for blood. We have to be damn careful from now on."

"I'm not surprised they found me, Max. In California yet? Any indication Howell found out about Tracy and Stephanie?"

"No! They appear to be unaware of the sisters as of yet, believing the Guerreros high-jacked Howell's boat for the cash on board. Smart money with my people says Howell's on his way to property he owns in Long Beach. That guy owns a shit load of properties in California. We're trying to identify them all."

"Woah! Man. That doesn't leave us a hell of-a lot of time to prepare a proper a reception."

"Furthermore," Max said, "the cartel's cancelled all deliveries out of Mexico. That put a crimp in DEA's plans."

Mike said, "What the hell brought that on?"

"We've known for a long time, but don't know where. Any communication between our drug enforcement and Mexican authorities goes straight to the cartels. We can't operate in Mexico without going through them first." He looked around at Mike. "Of course, you knew that, already."

"That definitely changes the game, Max. We're responsible for the women now. You know Howell's coming after me. So, if he finds the women here, he'll make them a priority. Their testimony would sink him."

"You're quite right, Mike. Are you still taking us ashore for breakfast? After that. I want everybody together for a review of your statements. We need to get that out of the way, then we should talk a bit before calling the shore-boat."

Mike looked up. "Good morning, Joel. How goes it this fine day?"

"Good to go, whaassup?"

"Max has some news. There's a lot going on."

Max washed down a bite of bagel with a large swallow of coffee. "I've no doubt you're all anxious to know what's to be done with that large sum of money recovered from the cartel."

Tracy said, "Didn't forget Max. We just pushed it aside. Didn't think it would work out for our benefit."

"Well, if you happen to generate a little interest. The FBI agreed to pay a reward for information leading to the disruption of a major drug distribution system funneling drugs into the US."

Max studied the girls. He admired their composure. "Once the investigation's completed each of you, Tracy, Stephanie, and Joel will receive a deposit into your retirement account. The net amount of $406,666. That will go into each account. Our negotiations with IRS determined accepting the funds in this manner would provide you with the greatest benefit. That's the best I could do."

The three participants stood staring at him. Obviously shocked, finding it hard to believe.

"Come on, say something," Mike said.

Max growled, "Now's the time for questions, or forever hold your peace. A letter from the IRS becomes part of your agreement. Believe me, the IRS share taken might have been much bigger."

Tracy and Stephanie jumped to their feet. Joel joined in, pulling them around and round. They laughed together, dragging Max and Mike into the melee.

Max stepped away. "Now don't go running your mouths off about this or the deal's off, ya hear?" He grinned.

Stephanie hugged Max, then kissed him on his cheek. "I never expected to have much more than an empty bank account. Thank you, Max."

Mike waved his arm dismissively toward Max. "Do you have anything casual in that small bag you brought aboard?"

"Not much, I plan to pick up a few things on shore."

"You'll be okay, just make sure you dump the coat and tie for the time being."

The crowded shore boat roared up to the rear of the big vessel, slowed at the last minute to ease against the swim platform. With standing room only, the operator yelled out, "Everybody, move close, hold her like you love her. Squeeze in tight for two additional pick-ups."

Mike pulled Tracy in tight against his body. The crowd swayed back and forth with the motion of the boat.

With a full load, the operator nudged the boat up against the dock on the pier. The noisy crowd scrambled up the ramp into the heart of Avalon.

"What a unique setting," Tracy said. "Right in the center of town. I wish we had time to walk around and look things over."

Stephanie moved to the outer railing after finishing her meal. She tossed breadcrumbs to an array of brightly colored fish swimming below. A fat seagull landed on the rail post near her. She and the big bird looked at each other for several moments before the bird reached over, plucked all the bread out of her hand and flew away.

"Darn that guy! Did you see him? I can't believe the audacity. No wonder he's so big and fat!"

Mike had to laugh. "Stephanie, you know they discourage feeding the seagulls."

"Shut up, Mike! You saw him take it right out of my hand." She laughed. "Do we have to leave so soon?"

She had the same deep laugh as Tracy. "Afraid so, Steph. We can make a quick stop on the way to the boat if anyone needs anything special," Mike said. "Okay then, let's hit the dock. Perhaps we can see more of Avalon at some point before returning to the real world. What do you think, Max?"

"We really don't have time to enjoy ourselves now. Maybe after I check in to see how things have developed."

Max made several calls from *Blue Dolphin*, then returned to share information he'd gathered. "Things have developed very fast overnight. Howell has a private detective from Mexico tracking Mike and Joel.

We have our men on them but haven't decided what action to take." *Everyone's getting panicky.*

Mike looked at the girls. "This can't be happening. That puts a whole different light on things. Is Howell's man on the island or the mainland?"

"As of now, he's in Long Beach. Howell has a condo there. Drug enforcement advises caution. They don't want us interfering with their plans. Their plan lets the narcotic operation start up again. They hope to catch the whole group in one big net. Tracy and Stephanie, you listen up. We don't know how this thing will play out. I want you both in a hotel here under my name. Joel, you'll stay there as well to look after the ladies."

Joel got up and paced. "Mike." He started to say more.

"Wait!" Max said. "Let me finish before your questions." He pointed at Mike. "You and I will move *Blue Dolphin* to Isthmus Harbor near the west end of the island to lead Howell and his thugs away from Tracy and Stephanie. Any connection between you ladies and Mike or the *Blue Dolphin* would mean an automatic death sentence for you. Because if he finds out you survived in Mexico, he knows that means his own death sentence. Howell's detective is well qualified and must not locate this boat and report the description of two women Howell would recognize in a heartbeat."

Mike said, "Then, we can't waste time. We need to get moving immediately. After we get the boat away from Avalon, it'll be safe for you to move around here without fear of recognition."

He looked at Max. "Better leave a tender for them don't you think? Moving around can often be safer than hiding in one place. Joel has a credit card. They all have cell phones."

He nodded at Joel. "You have a company credit card, Joel. Use it for yourself and both of our special ladies. There's no reason we can't stay in close contact."

Tracy grabbed Mike's arm. "Please be careful. I can't have anything happen to you, now that we've found each other again."

Max passed a business card to Joel. "Our people will let us know if the threat grows but it's important you memorize the sheriff's phone number. Are you okay with that?"

"Of course," Joel said. "You keep us in the loop and we'll do the same. How about you two? Will you be all right on the boat?"

Max spoke first. "Mike and I will be fine. You three probably won't need the help, but an undercover agent arrives in Avalon tomorrow morning to watch for trouble here. You won't meet him unless he feels a threat to you. He'll have your phone numbers."

Mike said, "Each of you pack what's needed and get going. We're moving to Two Harbors within forty-five-minutes. The sooner we get away the safer you'll be here."

Chapter 27

"You brought me into this mess, Mike. You may soon regret it," Max said. "You're under no further obligation to continue on in this fiasco. It's in our ball-park now. I hope you understand your yacht could suffer damage. You could even be injured."

Mike laughed. "Look, Max. This is all too important. You did say DEA found the evidence credible, the idea solid. So, let's move ahead. I understand what we're dealing with." *He likes keeping people off balance.*

"We're going big here, asking you for a strong commitment. I'm not sure you understand what you're into. Task Force Able has agents from the FBI, DEA, and a huge network of people inside Mexico, up the west coast, all the way to the Canadian border. You're only part of this operation because of your knowledge of the area and the depth of your recent involvement."

"I get it, Max. I agreed to play the part of a staked goat to draw Howell into the net. The sisters must be kept well away from the action."

"All right then. I'm aware of their importance as witnesses and their precarious situation. They'll be kept away from the danger area. If you're in, then quit sweating it, Mike. As your friend, I hate to see you involved with this mess at all."

"You have to know this by now, Max. I've given this a lot of thought. Wouldn't have suggested it otherwise. Go ahead, plant the story through your contacts in Mexico. The credible report of two women, last seen in a brawl at a restaurant in Cabo San Lucas on June tenth with known cartel members. That's a damn good reason for DEA operating in Mexico. We're willing to take our chances afterward."

"DEA agreed that's the direction to go, Mike. We will close the investigation and leak the information back through Mexican authorities. Then we wait and see if the drugs start flowing again." He scratched his head. "I'll needle task force leaders again to get the go-ahead."

"Now's the time to crap or get off the pot, Max. It's way too late for more brainstorming. Enough debate. Just make that call. The more I think about it, the more confidence I have in the plan. The facts back it up and the cartel has all the facts. Surely, TF leaders know that."

Max punched off the phone. "It's crucial that whereabouts of both sisters remain unknown to Howell for the success of our operation as well as their long-term safety. That uncertainty has delayed the decision-making process, Mike."

Mike didn't allow himself to visibly react. "Big trouble's coming. All these guys are bad news. We should get ourselves ready without the obvious security personnel onboard to give away the show."

"What're your thoughts on this guy, Howell?"

"I know he's a coward who loves to play the heavy with women, Max. I also know he's deadly. He'll hit hard with his goons along to make his part easy. He carries a knife and has experience using it. God, he's bad news. A real killer. Don't make the mistake of giving him half a chance. They'll come by dingy or other small boat between one and four in the morning, counting on catching us alone and sound asleep."

"All right, then. Let's give some thought to defending ourselves here on the yacht. Our people start undercover watches from midnight to eight in the morning, starting tonight. Agents will be riding with the harbor patrol boat. They'll have an unobstructed view of our vessel from one row back and two rows over, reporting all activity to me." He looked out at the nearby moorings. "My guess is they'll pick up our visitors soon as they show, if by boat. Our agent on the mainland has good eyes there. He's kept us well informed. Let's hope he continues updating."

"Thanks for your help, Max. There's time for a short swim to shake off the strain. You always kept yourself in good shape. There's nothing better than a swim to shake off some of this tension. I'm going to take a few laps around the boat. " He wondered if the old hip wound still gave Max trouble.

"That sounds good to me, old pal. Swimming's been my exercise of choice since that last frigging deployment. You have everything onboard, perhaps an extra swimsuit?"

"You have the choice of a warm-water dive suit or regular swimsuit. The water's fairly cold here near the west end of the island. We'll be okay for a half hour or so. Any longer and I'd suggest a lightweight dive suit. I'll go down and throw out a couple of options."

Mike returned in a Lycra swimsuit cut above the knee. Max hung up the phone, eying Mike. "How the hell do you hold onto all that muscle tone, Mike? I was impressed eight years ago. Now I'm even more impressed."

"A lifestyle, that's all. I run three miles every Tuesday, Thursday and Saturday. I work out on the heavy bag Monday and Wednesday, then rest up with a one-hour swim at five-thirty every morning that I'm home. It's a damn boring habit but I'm addicted, Max."

"You still teach hand-to-hand combat tactics to the officers in your reserve unit?"

"Yeah, a six-session course offered once a year to reserve officers willing to spend the time at regular meetings. A deadly serious undertaking. Not your normal self-defense tactics."

"What about women in your life? you must make time for that. As I recall, that was another one of your addictions."

"I see a few women, one a little more frequently than the others. There's no one special. I know what I want. It just hasn't been there for me. Starting to look better now. You still seeing that attorney in DC?"

"Nah, life got complicated and she moved on. I miss her."

Mike stepped up onto the safety railing with a hand on the radar arch. "We aren't going to be hit before late evening at the earliest. Let's get our swim in, and start the cocktail hour."

He turned briefly. "So, you know, Max. The Harbor Patrol boys, frown on swimmers in the fairways, they're not going to give us guff if we stay around our own vessel."

Mike descended to the rocky bottom forty feet below, turned his face upward and rose to the surface with a few slow kicks from long legs.

On the surface, Max said, "Go through your usual routine. I have my own. I know damn well I can't keep up with you."

Mike nodded. He dropped ten feet below the surface, swam the length of the *Blue Dolphin* twice before surfacing for a breath of air.

He thought about Howells's thugs and what might be expected. He knew Max would try to limit his exposure to risk. *Can't have that limit participation.*

He'll need me. Max faces task force bureaucracy, a hindrance to getting the drugs flowing again. Using the Cabo debacle as a reason for agents in Mexico is solid. He was certain Max's pressure would get things moving again.

Max put the phone down. "Howell's detective just left the island. He's been staked out on that hill above the USC research center since eleven this morning, giving us the eyeball with binoculars. Let's hope his report to Lance was favorable."

"There's no way Howell's gonna miss out on this chance at me, Max. We have to be ready for that."

In Port San Quinten, Augustine Palmira struggled to have packaged product ready to meet the next delivery. He'd not been able to reach Lance. Desperate for results, he called drug lord Federico Quanta with his problems. They were resolved quickly with new orders.

"We've lost confidence in Howell, Augustine. Can you handle things there without him?"

"That won't be a problem, Mr Rico. I know all the important contacts on both sides of the border."

"His problems with women have cost the organization time and money. We can't have that. I'll be in the Port San Quinten office by nine tonight. This could be profitable for you. We have a lot to talk about. You need not be concerned with Lance and his problems from now on. Just tend to our business, nothing else. Do you understand what I'm saying?"

Chapter 28

Mike kicked back with a cold beer, admiring a bikini clad blonde handling the mooring chores on an arriving sloop until he was interrupted by a call from Max.

Still pushing buttons on his cell, Max yelled, "Mike! Lance Howell and three very dangerous associates are headed our way with mayhem in mind."

"Yeah, shit's gonna hit the fan soon, tonight, I think. I know you have a plan, Max. Why don't you call your team onboard to get us all on the same page?"

"My thinking as well. It's time for a last-minute briefing. We need to know the good guys from the bad guys before the action starts."

Mike invited everyone into the main salon immediately after introductions for privacy.

"Hey, guys, the sun's beneath the yard-arm. With Max's permission the bar's open."

Max said, "This first." He leaned against the bar and looked at each man one by one. "In cooperation with the Harbor Patrol, undercover Agent Haskell, you and the DEA agents ride the harbor patrol boat. Flynn and Palmer, dressed as weekend fishermen, will join agent Alder on a sport fisher moored on the opposite side of *Blue Dolphin*."

Max smirked. "Listen up, now. Duty regulations regarding alcohol are tabled for the next hour. Duty starts at sundown. An open bar is too damn distracting. Drink judiciously."

With drink in hand, Max went on. "This bunch is damned dangerous, so don't get careless. Take them as petty thieves and you'll pay a heavy price. We have to stop them from entering this vessel at the instant of boarding. We make arrests at that time and not a minute before, understand?"

Agent Palmer spoke up. "Are you sure they won't turn and head back to the fishing boat, or try to make a run for it? That's about what you'd expect from these dirt bags."

Another agent waved his hand around. "Once we identify ourselves, the futility of running should be obvious. Our drawn weapons should trump whatever they have."

"Don't be so sure of that. Things won't happen that easily. Lance Howell and Big Jake Hayward smell blood. Mike's blood. It's personal. They're expected to be coming in with the attacking crew. Both have too much to lose. Either one will kill you or be killed before he gives in to an easy arrest."

Mike leaned away from the bar. "Gentlemen, I know this guy Howell. He's known to use a knife. I expect that to be their choice of weapons, less noisy."

Max picked up again. "Don't expect an arrest before one or both men get seriously injured. We have a hard confrontation ahead tonight. Make sure you wear your vest and any other protective gear that's available. Even if you find yourself in the water, it may help against knife slashes. Are there any non-swimmers present? No? That's a positive. Some of us may find ourselves swimming before this thing's over.

"Mike, you're the intended target. I want you up top, as far away from Howell's knife as possible, at least to begin with. Agent Haskell. You and your two agents from D.E.A. will utilize the heavy RIB to block forward motion of the attacking boat. Nose up to the front of their dingy as fast as possible. Agent Flynn. You and Agent Palmer utilize the harbor patrol boat to block them from the rear.

Max said with a wink, "Me, myself, Max and I, along with my trusty Sig will remain on the lower deck to prevent entry onto the yacht. Remember. When the action begins, have weapons drawn and ready. It's most important to remain in constant contact and stay quiet until the action starts. Be ready to move once the attackers approach the boarding area of *Blue Dolphin*. I'll key all mics at that point. Move in quickly. Until then, we'll keep out of sight. Do absolutely nothing to give your position away."

The meeting ended quickly. Mike shook hands with each man. "Good luck. It's my pleasure to work with you gentlemen."

Max grabbed his arm. "Let's you and me have a look around the area from above, where you'll start out. You can observe and report from there."

At sundown, they watched agents Flynn and Palmer begin a slow patrol of the area outside the harbor.

Soon after ten thirty, Max received a report from Agent Palmer.

Mike listened intently to the conversation. He picked up high resolution glasses and followed a fishing boat with several large men onboard approach the anchorage.

Max clicked off to call the harbor patrol boat. He suggested they position the fishing boat where it could be under constant observation by agents.

Within minutes, Mike made the first positive ID. "Max! That's Big Jake Hayward, spitting image of the wanted poster." Moments later he saw a rubber dingy launched, and head into the harbor with one person onboard. From his high position on the bridge, Mike tracked the man in the small boat. He passed everything to Max who relayed it to the other agents.

Agents Haskell and Carter continued to watch the men in the fishing boat. They called out a positive ID on all but Lance Howell.

Max said, "You don't suppose he sent these guys to do his dirty work alone, do you?"

"No way, Max! This is too personal. He wants my blood. I believe he's keeping a low profile for the time being. He'll pop up like a bloated fish carcass soon as the action starts. Let's grab a six-pack of beer and sit in the cockpit acting like everyone else until that guy feels comfortable."

The lone individual in the rubber dingy motored around the boats moored inside the harbor, sometime gliding past where Mike and Max sat, close enough to nod a 'hello'. At last, after resting at the pier-side dock for thirty minutes, he headed straight back outside the harbor. He passed close enough to slide his fingers along the slick side of *Blue Dolphin*.

Mike looked at his dive watch. *Past midnight. Won't be long now*. He donned a thick, above the knee, short-sleeved wetsuit, answered a call from Max, then strapped a razor-sharp dive knife to his right calf and entered the salon.

He placed the still active telephone on the bar, in speaker mode. "What the hell are you up to, Mike? We don't have time to play games. There are four extra big men headed our way in that little rubber dingy."

"I'm prepared to end up in the water if need be. You'd better get yourself ready as well, Max. I don't expect action until after they check out everything around us. We'd better stay out of sight for a while longer." He watched Max disappear into the salon, the only entrance to the yacht through the open cockpit. He flattened himself on the upper sundeck with a good view of surroundings. He watched the men in the dingy pass close by and passed it on to Max. From his high position he watched the rubber dingy circle around *Blue Dolphin* again. He watched them look around the open decks, and move away slowly. They motored on toward where DEA. agents were hunkered down in the sport fisher, prepared for action. The heavy load created a wake large enough to rock the smaller boats nearby.

Mike called again. "They're getting impatient, Max. It could happen anytime now. They're looking closely at the boarding area. Ready your men. They're headed this way, slowing down, Max. Yes. They're eyeballing the landing area." Then louder, "It's a go! Max, go, go, go. Now Max, now!"

Chapter 29

Fast moving agents converged on the men in the rubber boat, but not fast enough. Two large men leaped onto the swim platform with weapons. They ran through the cockpit toward Max.

He shouted, "Federal Agents! Drop your weapons." He yelled again, "Federal Agents! Hands in the air."

Agents from both teams pointed weapons at the men in the boat. They shouted out, "Federal Agents. Hands in the air!"

Demands were ignored. Poor light caused agents to delay firing for fear of hitting their own.

Howell's men grasped the advantage when two of his men jumped into the vessel with DEA agents, slashing agents in the boat with filet knives, creating confusion in the dark.

Mike flipped a switch, flooding the area with bright light. He saw two men ignore the order and attack Max. One big man near Max swung a steel pipe. It struck Max's hand holding the gun. The weapon fired, missed center mass, where intended, shattered the assailant's left collar bone, and exited the back. He fell against the port rail, hurt, not out of the fight.

Mike dropped into the cockpit. He yelled at a man moving in on Max with a knife, held low, blade flat. *A throat-slash, Lance.* He shouted, "Hey woman beater!"

Mike moved in fast, faked a kick, dodged a swipe with the knife, stepped to one side and raked a razor-sharp dive knife across Lance's knife wielding upper arm. He felt the blade strike bone, knew tendons had been cut. The knife fell to the deck. He saw the big man near the rail go for Max's gun. He ran three steps, slammed him hard, taking both over the railing into the dark water.

Mike popped up quickly. He looked around. He heard shouting from the RIB, saw a violent knife fight in the inflatable. He slipped under the water, came up next to the boat. Lance's man held an agent tight against his body, slashing at another agent in the boat. Mike reached up from the water, slashed the cutting arm of the assassin, grabbed him by the hair and dragged him over into the water. The agent in the bottom of the boat fired once, hitting the remaining assassin in the forehead, sending him over the side. *Let the bastard sink,* Mike thought.

He looked for Max on board *Blue Dolphin*, couldn't see him. He swam toward where Max had been seen fighting. He passed Big Jake in the water, straining to hold onto the rubber boat drifting free. He climbed aboard the yacht, rushed into the main salon. He found

Max warding off a weakened, still violent Lance Howell, who'd recovered his knife and continued to attack with one arm. Max held him at bay with the aid of a long-handled deck brush.

Mike yelled, "Lance! you son-of-a-bitch! Don't know when to tap out, do you?"

Lance turned toward Mike and received a powerful blow to the rib cage from Mike's left leg. *Sounded like a repeat of Cabo, the same three ribs breaking.* Instead of falling to the deck, Lance fell against a large bait tank and remained standing. He positioned his knife for another attack, breathing hard.

Mike yelled, "Drop the knife, Lance."

"Don't really think so. I ain't done yet." He lunged at Mike, slashing wildly.

Mike stepped forward, fainted a left to the head and severed Lance's left bicep, leaving both arms useless.

Lance lowered himself to the bloody deck and stared at Mike McGowin. "You bastard."

Mike turned away, looking for Max. He saw him pick up the knife and toss it overboard.

FBI agents assisted the wounded DEA agents. Max ordered a one-armed survivor to remain where he was, holding a grab line from the drifting RIB. He pointed farther out. "Look at that! Big Jake's trying to slip away in the dark."

Mike said, "Don't let anyone shoot me, Max!" He dived into the dark water, remained under, then popped to the surface near a bow line hanging from the rubber boat. He towed the boat back toward Max and the other agents, then realized Big Jake had pulled himself into the boat and began yanking on the starting cord to the small outboard motor using his one good arm.

Mike released the tow line, reached up with his knife, making long cuts in both floatation chambers, one side and then the other. He swam back to where agents were watching.

Big Jake sat struggling in the sinking boat.

Mike yelled from the water, "There are medical kits in each stateroom, Max, with another larger one on the bridge."

"We found some, Mike. I think we'll need more if we hope to save Lance and your other slash victim."

Agent Flynn towed the sinking RIB back to the yacht with Big Jake floundering inside. With one arm useless for swimming, he appeared submissive.

Mike leaned over the sinking RIB to help agents remove the three-hundred-pound man from the water filled boat. He reached for the heavy belt. Suddenly a strong arm grabbed him around his neck, pulling him overboard. He knew struggling would only tire him out. He took in a deep breath, felt himself being pulled down deep into the water between the two boats.

Agents above watched, unable to assist. A full minute passed. Agents stared at the black water.

Mike concentrated on dim light above. Exhausted, he reached up, felt for the mooring line. He heard someone yelling, sensed his head break the surface. He hung on to the line, taking in great breaths of air.

"I need a little assistance here with this dead weight, fellows." He lifted his other hand enough to show he gripped a thick ankle with an enormous foot attached.

Two uninjured agents quickly leaned down, taking charge of the heavy body. They maneuvered it over to the swim platform where help waited.

Max yelled out, "How the hell did you manage that? We thought for sure a recovery effort was going to be needed. I've seen you in the water enough to have some hope, but even I was beginning to have my doubts."

"I simply relaxed, Max. Until he loosened his grip around my neck. He twitched a few times and drifted away. It was pure luck I felt a big foot on my first effort to reach out. It was necessary to change hands on the way up, he's so damned heavy. I almost released him before seeing the glow above. He should have taken better care of himself."

Max came back to where Mike rested in the cockpit. "Agent Haskell and two D.E.A. agents have been hurt, one with serious injuries. Everyone was cared for on the teak deck of your main salon. We used most of your medical supplies, Mike. One of your victims just died from loss of blood at the triage station. We think it was

Lance Howell. His remains, along with other dead, have been moved to the Coast Guard boat."

He passed mike a bottle of water. I asked sheriff's deputies and Harbor Patrol officers to arrest the fleeing fishing boat captain. He was picked up less than a mile from the Two Harbors anchorage. A U.S. Coast Guard cutter from San Pedro arrived in time to assist in the arrest.

Mike sat quietly watching curious boaters gathered on deck taking in the bright lights and noisy harbor activity. He knew harbor patrol officers had spread a story of an attempted boat hijacking for the gawkers. He listened patiently to Max interact with officials. At last, he poured fresh coffee and began settling down.

Max turned off his phone and joined him with coffee. He'd arranged an afternoon flight off the island with the Coast Guard, then a flight to Washington.

"You've made some new friends very happy, old friend of mine. Relax and finish your coffee while I prepare to get us underway. It'll be daylight when we reach Avalon."

Max said, "This thing isn't over, old-pal until the fat lady sings. I have weeks of work ahead, thanks to you."

"I'm sure you do. Documentation and justification on this caper's gonna choke a horse."

In Port San Quinten, Mexico, Augustine Palmira felt the pressure of his new job. He talked with Federico Quanta, for the third time in one day.

He stressed over new orders. "Push delivery up one day earlier than planned, Augustine. The threat is no longer there. No human cargo this time. Load every bit of product available. It's badly needed across the border in California. Call in extra help if necessary. I want everything we have on the way north. The mothership will be waiting for the rendezvous."

Chapter 30

Tracy shifted her position to face away from the morning sun. The small open air restaurant overlooking Avalon Harbor was crowded with boaters. "So, we agreed to play tourist today, let Joel share his local knowledge, and drive us around in one of those little open air jeep style vehicles. Right, Joel?"

"You two finish your morning coffee while I make a deal for one of those vehicles. That's the only way to get around the island. You'll love the view of the harbor from the Wrigley Mansion. That's just one thing you should see. We need a vehicle that's not completely worn out. They're very popular and the newer ones go first."

"Don't rush, Joel. I'd rather not leave this choice people watching spot. We may have a Bloody Mary while waiting. It's a nice break just sitting here, looking at the boats and watching all the people walk by. We'll work on our tan some more while you're gone."

Stephanie said, "I don't know about you, Tracy. I'm having a hard time facing reality. This past week has been something between a nightmare and a fantasy.

An exciting dream in many ways. I feel so guilty, then so very grateful to everyone. You, Mike and Joel all risked everything to find me and stop those horrible men. I'd given up after you disappeared. The last few weeks, we've been part of one miracle after another. Neither of us ever put a great deal of emphasis into our Christian religion, did we?"

Tracy shook her head. "I'm like you about religion. I've always taken it for granted. After everything that's happened, all the near misses and amazing things we've experienced, I see things different. It was more than just luck. Our survival, I mean. It really was a miracle. Maybe there's a greater deity. Mike came back into my life, fulfilling my dreams. Both our lives have been spared, along with the unexpected financial security that may come with it. It's a second chance at life, sis. For both of us. I know people wouldn't believe what we've been through. Just think about Mom and Dad. Not knowing was really hard on both." She stopped to think about the new beginning with Mike. She hoped they could make things work as a family. Now, she worried about the danger facing him, the unknown.

Joel parked one street back from the waterfront and walked to where the girls were. He paid their tab. "We don't have a lot of time, ladies. You should see the view from the Wrigley Mansion first. If time allows, we can visit the Zane Grey house next, then the gardens, near the old-time Chicago Cubs practice field, before visiting some of the more interesting shops."

Tracy said, "What's the rush? Don't we have all day?"

"We do, but the glass bottom boat ride and the trip inland through the buffalo herd will take up the afternoon. We'll be busy all day."

The day had been fun but tiring. Tracy had trouble sleeping. Being with Mike all week brought back the deep caring and intensity of the hurt she'd forced on herself so long ago. She couldn't stop thinking about the danger facing him now. Why hasn't she heard something?

She'd been awakened by her cell. "Thank you, Joel. Do you mind if Steph and I hang here at the hotel this morning? We'll meet you for lunch at Eric's, on the pier. I'd like to try those buffalo burgers you were bragging about if that's OK. We'll meet you there at noon."

She showered fast, avoided waking Steph and went downstairs to the sidewalk coffee-bar. She was surprised at the number of people out walking so early. She turned heads sitting alone at a table near the busy sidewalk dressed in white shorts and halter. She considered moving farther back so she could stretch her long legs out without attracting attention.

Anxiety ate away at her nerves. She'd felt that way since Mike left for the expected confrontation. Not knowing or hearing anything at all only made matters worse. She desperately wanted to know what had happened during the night. She expected only the worst. *Why punish myself with negative thoughts?* She decided a short walk along the harbor front would relieve the tension.

She felt her phone vibrate. Joel again. He'd just received a call from Mike. They were on their way back to Avalon. There had been bad trouble at Two Harbors. They were all OK. *Why wouldn't they give us more information?*

Erick's Café on the pier proved to be crowded with people. She couldn't remain seated. She asked Steph to hold their table, picked up her beer, moved across the pier to lean against the railing. She stared down at a world of colorful fish flashing through the clear water, then stared down at the few sun worshipers lying on the small beach below. *I have to do something with this nervous energy,* she thought.

Joel appeared and waved her over. The three friends tied up a small table on the busy pier and watched the hustle and bustle of small tenders loaded with people move between vessels in the harbor. All three talked nervously, ate buffalo burgers and drank cold Mexican beer, anxious for news. The last phone call had them speculating about no less than stories of mayhem the night before at the other end of the island. They agreed. Not knowing made waiting worse.

Joel answered his phone again. Another call from Mike. "They're only a few minutes away from the harbor." He rushed to the counter and ordered four buffalo burgers to go. "Max had better be quick or Mike will eat all four of these things. You've seen him eat, haven't you?"

Tracy jumped to her feet. "Oh yeah! You should see him in a steak house, Joel. Do you mind if we rush on down and wait for you in the tender? I can't sit still. I'm anxious for details they wouldn't share with us over the phone. One of them could be injured and we wouldn't even know."

Joel caught up with Tracy and Stephanie. "Tracy, you're as nervous as the nursing home's long-tailed cat in a room full of rockers. You aren't happy to see that big guy, are you?"

She laughed. "I've struck gold, Joel. It's not the bank account either. I made a huge mistake hurting Mike as well as myself the first time around. Can't lose him again, regardless of anything else that might happen."

Bright sunlight reflected off the water making it hard to distinguish details on board the vessel. They'd stopped in the outer harbor waiting for the harbor patrol escort.

"Why wait here, let's go," Joel said.

He dropped Tracy and Stephanie off onto the swim platform and moved away to wait for the vessel to enter the harbor.

Max hugged each woman with one arm, the other heavily wrapped, resting in a sling.

Stephanie noticed the injury. "Max! What in the world is wrong with your hand?"

"All's okay, Stephanie. Hold on while I give Tracy a hand up."

"I've never been happier to see someone," Tracy said. "*Blue Dolphin* looked like a ghost ship coming out of the mist."

Mike waited on the bridge for Tracy and Stephanie. He kissed Stephanie on the cheek, lifted Tracy off her feet to place a firm kiss on her lips.

Stephanie pummeled Max with questions. "You've had trouble. Tell us what's going on."

Mike said, "Hold on, there's lots to tell. Let us hook up to the mooring first."

Joel couldn't wait. He tied the tender alongside and rushed onboard to deliver a brown bag and a six-pack of cold beer to the salon. "Hey, guys, there's buffalo burgers in the bag."

Tracy said, "Come on, guys, give with what's been happening. We can see there's been a fight. Sit down and talk while we listen. You're entitled to a little pampering."

She gathered potato chips from a food storage locker with plastic plates, napkins for each. She hurriedly placed two buffalo burgers and a beer on a tray and delivered one to each weary looking man.

She motioned to Stephanie, then backed away to look at Mike's unshaven face. "Look at Mike, Steff. He looks almost as scary as that big unshaven man that dragged me off that patch of seaweed in Mexico." Her eyes teared up. She kissed him on the cheek and sat down, close against him.

Max swallowed a mouthful of burger before speaking. "OK, ladies. Being tired is no excuse. I'm aware of the terrible ordeal inflicted upon you two young women. Lance Howell will not be around to terrify any other women." He looked from one to the other. "For that reason, you deserve to know how his life ended."

He related, in graphic detail, the story of what happened at Two Harbors. "Howell almost made it. At the very end, he bled out on board a small boat carrying him to a triage station set up on the pier by the Coast Guard."

Stephanie grimaced, shaking her head. She explained again briefly how she'd been taken in by that smooth-talking, attractive man she first met at a beach volleyball tournament in Santa Barbara.

Tracy hooked her arm under Max's good arm. "Max, what do you plan to do now? I hope you'll be able to stay around for a few days. You deserve a break."

"There's too much unfinished business, Tracy. It can only be handled from Washington. I've arranged to be picked up at five p.m. from the old sea plane terminal. Coast Guard has provided a helicopter ride to LAX for an evening flight into Dulles International near Washington, D.C. We need to finish this job while everything's in motion. There's a great deal more work to be done."

Max went below long enough for a quick shower and shave. He returned showing his tiredness, ready to travel, holding the discarded coat and tie.

Tracy reached up and kissed him lightly. "I feel like we're all family here, Max. I'm sure you're aware that Mike's the father of my daughter Catherine. I haven't been asked yet, but I'm going to marry him. Can I count on you at our wedding?"

"I'd never miss your wedding, Tracy. If he gives you any trouble, let me know and I'll have him arrested, so you and I can tie the knot instead. Remember. A little snow on the roof doesn't mean there's not a fire in the furnace."

Mike spun Tracy around. He dropped to one knee and placed both hands together beneath his chin. "Tracy, I've been crazy in love with you since we first met. Will you marry me?"

She backed away. "I don't know. Are you sure, Mike? I do have another offer waiting you know." She grinned at Max, pushed Mike over onto the deck and sat on him. "I accept. I also want sworn statements from all the witnesses here."

Stephanie said, "Let him up, Tracy. You need to help me with the wine. We have to celebrate with a toast before Max's shore boat arrives."

Max said, "I'll drink to each one of you several times on the flight home. You've made a wise decision to marry that man, Tracy."

Mike led Max outside for a few words with his close friend. "I believe my part of this thing is over. You will keep me in the loop, won't you? All the way to the finish? I'm grateful to you, Max, for all you've done here."

Max wrapped his arm around Mike. "No, thank you for bringing this thing to us, old buddy. I knew I could count on you for a little excitement. Somehow, Mike. Your troubles always involve beautiful women. You haven't changed a damn bit."

Chapter 31

Mike saw an SUV drive into the guest parking at Marina Del Rey Yacht Club. He finished off the beer he'd been nursing and moved for a better view. He smiled inwardly when a pretty little girl rushed past a tall man to look out in his direction. *That must be Catherine. She's beautiful.* "Tracy! Come up, now! I believe they're here."

Moments later, Stephanie and Tracy blew past Mike out into the open arms of Harold and Mickey Conwell, standing on the gangway.

Mike kept his eye on Catherine as she wrapped her arms around her mother. He marveled at hearing his daughter's voice for the first time. "Does my daddy live here?"

"No, sweetheart. This is a yacht club where people keep their big boats," Mickey said. "Your daddy has a guest slip here for today and tomorrow so we can all get to know each other." Catherine released her grip on her mother and turned to look at Mike.

He hurried out to greet her and dropped down on one knee to be eye level with Catherine. She appeared shy at first, then rushed into his arms.

"I'm so sorry, honey. It's taken a long time, hasn't it?"

She seemed shy but curious. Her spoken words sounded like a grownup speaking.

"Are you, my dad?"

He nodded and cradled her in his arms. He continued to hold her like a tiny tot, both afraid to say more. *She's mature, so much family resemblance.* They moved into the salon together. He asked her how she liked LA. How she liked school there. She talked about playing soccer and wanting to try out for basketball later. They stayed near until time to turn and meet Mr and Mrs Conwell. He hugged Mickey warmly. Used his left hand to greet Hal. He turned again to holding Catherine against him until Tracy called her over.

He kneeled to give her a tender kiss. "Go on with Mom and Gramma, honey. We will always be close now. I'll see you again in a few minutes."

Mike and Hal slipped away for a few moments of privacy. Hal said, "Thank you, Mike. I'm not an overly religious man but I believe you were placed there in the right place at the right time for the specific purpose of saving the girls from a horrible death. We will never be able to thank you enough. When we have another moment of privacy, I would appreciate the details of

Tracy and Stephanie's stressful period of captivity prior to rescue."

Mike felt a strange familiarity with Hal. He admired Hal's sincerity. "I'm a beneficiary of all that's happened Hal. We're going to have ample opportunity to go over everything." He put an arm around Hal and they returned to the others.

Tracy held her mother's hand. "Aren't you glad to be here aboard the yacht with us?"

"It's very nice, honey. We weren't sure about being away for more than one night." She laughed. "That was some heavy lobbying by you and Mike that brought this about. Hal and I have never been aboard any boat overnight."

Mike looked at his watch. "Cocktail hour must commence soon, with only one short hour before our dinner reservations at the Warehouse restaurant."

Stephanie and Tracy took over bar duties. Stephanie pulled out a bottle of white wine for herself and Tracy.

Mike spoke up. "How about a good scotch, Hal?"

"It's about time, and a martini for Mickey. She isn't called Martini Mickey without good reason. And Mike, I like any man that appreciates good scotch."

"Well, sis, looks like you and I are having a glass of wine, all by ourselves," Stephanie said.

Mickey raised her martini glass. "Thank you, Mike, for looking after our girls."

Hal nodded at Mike. "You have my grateful appreciation as well."

"Thank you both for your warm acceptance. I love Tracy very much. I've always loved her. Is it OK with you if we get married immediately?"

Hal looked at Tracy. "You love him?"

"Of course I do! Remember what I said to you and Mom, so long ago? Only time has changed. My feelings have not."

Hal raised his glass again. "Welcome to our family. I regret it's taken so long, Mike. You've made Tracy very happy."

Tracy pulled her parents in closer together. Her eyes glistened with tears. "You both have always been there for me. Without you, Catherine and I could not have held out. Now we have Mike who also loves us. Thank you, Mom and Dad, for making it all possible. I really do believe in miracles now."

Mike picked Catherine up again. He placed a light kiss on the tip of her nose and sat down with her. She turned to face him. They held eye contact for a long moment. "Your mom and I are getting married right away so we can be a real family like I've always wanted."

Catherine's face lit up. "Will we all live together like Gramma and Poppa?"

"Yes, sweetheart. You, Mom and I will always be together now. Is that okay with you?"

"I can't wait for my friends to meet you. I want to call you Dad. Is it okay?"

"It sure is, honey. I want to show you off to my friends too. You'll soon get to meet your cousins, who'll love you. And you'll also be meeting Grandpa Marcus, my dad. He can't wait to meet you! When school starts, can I go with you the first day?"

"Sure, Dad. I hope you will, and maybe Mom too."

They were late for dinner at the Warehouse. Mike ordered champagne poured for another round of toasts. He insisted Catherine be seated between himself and Tracy.

Tracy tapped a spoon against her glass. "Listen up, everyone. Mike's been in touch with his family. He's worked out a family gathering. It'll be a casual, relaxed setting at his dad's house in Mandalay Bay. He would like our two families to become close. He wants the gathering right away."

Mike said, "My father reserved time at the Pacific Corinthian Yacht Club in Channel Islands Harbor for a family get-together. Tracy and I felt it important to have everyone get acquainted as soon as possible. Dad's very excited. He'll be thrilled to have Tracy and Catherine staying with me. My mom would have loved them."

Chapter 32

Mike McGowin looked down Santa Monica Boulevard from his fifth-floor office. He turned away from the window and looked at a folded-up blueprint on his desk. *That can wait another day, maybe two after tomorrow,* he thought.

He wondered what afternoon traffic on coast highway would be like. An hour at the beach with his new family this evening would be nice.

The day had started early at a Van Nuys construction site. He'd confronted a combative general contractor who insisted on cutting corners at their new fifty thousand square foot low-rise office complex. The shoddy work gained the attention of the anchor tenant. Not acceptable. Mike had issued a last warning before leaving for Mexico.

"No more deviations from the contract, Halloran. Core samples prove you poured the most recent ten thousand square feet of ground level flooring with less than first grade concrete. I may have you jack hammer it out and replace it. This on top of the long list of problems we gave you last week."

"You're just a hard ass, McGowin. I've been in this business for twenty years and nobody's ever questioned my work like you do. I have to take all of this up with Sweeney. He's always been happy with my work."

"You do that! And remember, the anchor tenant is complaining about the cheap cabinetwork in the executive suites. He's watching everything you do because he's thinking of buying the building. He may demand replacement of those cabinets as well. And Halloran. No more cost overruns without signed changes to the work order. As far as your twenty years of experience, it must have been one year, experienced twenty times. Swenco has been notified that progress payments will be delayed until I sign off on all work from this point forward."

Damn. Now he knew why this guy never ran one of McGowin's jobs before. *Swenco must be having trouble*. The bid was not awarded to them because of low price. Quality from this contractor which had the winning bid, but not the low bid, was paramount. As McGowin Corporation's Executive vice president for engineering, design and construction, Mike had never allowed short cuts or lower grade materials.

He took time to cool down, stretched his back muscle some more, then shifted his efforts to a second major project taking up much of his time. He leaned over a large print table for an hour, compared progress at the construction site to drawings for the remodel of the ninety thousand square foot Wilshire property. The older building has needed attention for a long time. The improvement brought it up to date and helped retain some of the legacy firms up for renewal.

Mike strolled down the hall to the office of his sister Sally, age thirty-eight, chief financial officer of McGowin Corporation. Then through the accounting office where several people were busy at computers, working their magic. He nodded and smiled warmly at Ann, Sally's secretary and walked directly to Sally's long leather couch. He stretched himself out, taking up the full length of the furniture.

Sally hung up the phone. "How's the back?"

"It's OK, Sal. I did a little too much bending over the drafting table today."

"OK then! Let's get to the important stuff, your new family."

Sally walked around and sat on the corner of her desk. "One more thing, Mike. You have a lot on your plate. I'm concerned about the Swenco project."

Mike turned back from the door. "I've made the decision to have the construction superintendent replaced with another man we've worked with in the past. That's their only chance to save themselves. I spoke to Sweeney an hour ago."

Mike had another early morning walkthrough at the construction site. He arrived late for the special board meeting. Never shy about walking through the corporate office in work clothes (often blue jeans, tee shirt and heavy work shoes), he rushed down a hallway past his own office and into the executive locker rooms for a quick shower and change of clothes. The chairman was a stickler for the corporate dress code at all board functions.

He tucked in a freshly laundered shirt, tightened his tie and pulled on a tailored light grey Italian suit jacket. He passed Ann again on his way to the boardroom.

She said, "Good morning, Mike," without looking. "Your sisters are waiting for you in the boardroom."

He was greeted by other staff members as he hurried through the office.

"Well, look what the cat dragged in!" Sally said, as he entered the boardroom. "I wonder if the board would take you seriously if they saw you thirty minutes ago in your usual attire." Several board members greeted the late arrival in a friendly manner.

"Fortunately, he cleans up well," Gayle said.

"Thank you, ladies. All in the line of duty."

Gayle and Sally finished up with a variety of issues of interest to the board.

Sally asked, "Did you talk to Joel? He's still having relationship problems with Swenco and their quality control issues."

"I talked with him on the way here after talking to Sweeney. That's one general contractor that has one last chance to straighten up. After receiving a cease-and-desist order while we were in Mexico, their work improved only moderately. I've arranged a change of the superintendent. The back-up sub-contractors lined up to finish the job will not be necessary. Joel's documented problems and shortcuts were obvious to the management team reviewing the work. Halloran couldn't get the job done. He's gone after tomorrow."

The board meeting was called to order. Chairman of the board, Marcus McGowin, addressed Mike. "Those issues requiring board approval should be brought forward now, Mike. Some of the other members and I have another pressing meeting to attend before noon. We'll address these issues and take our leave."

Mike presented the design revisions and new cost estimates for a previously approved forty-five-unit apartment complex to be built next year in Santa Monica. Also requiring board approval was the purchase of a five-acre tract of raw land in North Malibu. After a brief discussion, approval was granted. Other less critical new projects were pushed back until next year.

A productive meeting with no further business before the board, a motion to adjourn was made. That was seconded and carried. The board members departed.

"Well, Gayle. Our old-time construction foremen and property managers have done well keeping you up to date here in the corporate offices while Joel and I were transiting up and down the coast of Baha. Of course, we scorched the telephone system staying in touch with project foremen."

He looked from Gayle to Sally. "As you know, all our people have been with us for many years. They're loyal to the company. We trust their judgment, and best of all, they are highly responsible." He grinned at his sisters. "Otherwise, I wouldn't have been able to leave work for several weeks for a family outing in Mexico."

Chapter 33

Joel eased *Blue Dolphin* against the hundred-foot dock at the McGowin home in Mandalay Bay. The corner lot, mostly taken up by the three-story main house and guest house, left only a thirty-foot strip of green lawn between the sea wall and rear parking area. A drive through beneath the guest house accommodated parking for four cars on a concrete apron between home and water. The quiet approach of *Blue Dolphin* caught Barbara Blair and Marcus McGowin unaware. Barbara heard voices coming from people lining the yacht's railing. She and Marcus had been having coffee on an eastside nook near the kitchen. Barbara alerted Marcus and they rushed out to greet the new arrivals.

Mike led Catherine up the ramp toward Marcus, with Tracy at his side. The others followed along the flagstone walk leading into a shaded patio where everyone could exchange greetings. Barbara Blair went directly to Catherine. She reached out, smiling. "Hi, Catherine. I'm Barbara and this is your other grandfather. He'd like for you to call him Papa or Papa Marcus. But first, he wants a great big hug."

Mike tugged Tracy over to face his dad. "And this is Tracy, the mother of our daughter Catherine, and more future grandchildren for you, Dad. She's forever the love of my life. Please don't smother her with that beard. I'd like to keep her around for a while." Tracy moved closer to the huge, bearded man now holding Catherine against his hip. A long arm encircled her shoulders, pulling her tight against a solid body.

"You two have made me the happiest, and luckiest man in the world, Tracy. I intend to love you both so much it may make your mother and father jealous."

Hal spoke up. "I'm already feeling the pain, Marcus. These two have been such an important part of our lives. I'm Tracy's father. This is my wife, Mickey. It looks like we've gained a son! We didn't waste time. We've already adopted Mike into our family."

Marcus embraced Hal and Mickey, each in turn. "Welcome to the McGowin family, Hal. My home and heart will always be open to you both."

Stephaney nudged her dad. He put his arm around her.

"Marcus, this is our other daughter, Stephanie. You already know the full story. We're forever grateful to Mike and Joel who rescued our daughters. There courage and tenacity throughout the ordeal was amazing."

"You should be proud of your girls as well. They confronted the devil face to face and helped render justice the old-fashioned way."

"Thank you. The loss of our two daughters would've been tragic. We would never recover from such a loss."

Barbara, Marcus's assistant, moved everyone into the open family room. "There's a wonderful view of the harbor while waiting for refreshments," she said.

"Please relax here with Marcus while I open up the guest house. You'll be able to rest there and freshen up before dinner at the club. You'll need a break before and after with this family."

Phil and Sally Robinson arrived with their children, Samantha and Brett. With them were Bob and Gayle Alder and their daughters, Sara and Tanya.

The Crow's Nest at the Yacht Club and shaded portion of the outside deck were reserved for the McGowin party.

Mike said, "Come on, Phil. Let's see what Dad ordered up in the way of good wine." He knew Marcus was listening. "We may want to stick with a Coors."

Marcus laughed. "I heard that. All you childish beer drinkers may decide to give up beer all together, after tasting my choice wines. Try these favorites of mine. A 2016 Dark Star Anderson Road that's been breathing for about an hour, or the Hunt Cellars 2014 Syrah. Both are excellent." He laughed. "Don't bother with the Hunt wines unless you have a refined taste."

He tapped his glass. "Ask those standing outside to step in for a toast. We rarely have these family gatherings since Marie passed." He raised his glass.

"Let us lift our glasses once more to the Conwell family. And the return of their beautiful daughters."

He waved a huge hand. "Also! A long life together for Mike and Tracy. May the bond be permanent, the future bountiful, and life's journey filled with joy."

Harold Conwell raised his glass. "To the McGowins and their warm welcome. Thank you, Marcus!"

Mike's cell phone vibrated. He went outside to get away from the music. "Yes, this is Mike."

"This is Bruce Briggs, Mr McGowin, with your home security service. At nine-forty-five this evening, we received a signal here alerting us to a breach of the alarm system on the west patio of your Calabasas home. We alerted the local police and sent our nearest roving patrolman to have a look. Soon after, we received a call from the Calabasas police officer arriving on scene. He reported that our security patrolman had been ambushed and killed, just outside the damaged entrance to your house. The police officers are requesting your presence at the scene."

Chapter 34

Mike removed a nine-millimeter Sig Sauer semi-automatic handgun and two full mags of ammunition from his father's heavy wall mounted gun safe. He racked the slide a few times, inserted a full mag into the butt, racked back one more time to place a round in the chamber. There's no safety lever on this weapon. The safety feature is the trigger finger and brain of the user.

Moments later, he released his belt buckle and single button at the top of his fly on a portion of his old military uniform. He allowed the baggy utility pants to fall around his ankles. He stepped away, retrieved a wide, thin elastic belt with a six-inch vertical slit, to the right of center, pulled it tight around his hips below the belt line and engaged the Velcro. He refastened his trousers, held the sig in his right hand, used his left hand to open the fly, placing two fingers into the slit. He stretched the opening out and slid the weapon inside, a maneuver he'd practiced many times while serving his country. Mike often carried an undeclared weapon into meetings with so called friendlies.

By midnight, he neared the end of the forty-five-minute drive to the scene of the killing. *What the hell is going on? This can't be coincidental. There must be a connection to the drug smuggling operation. Why else at my home?*

He entered the private drive leading to the ten-acre family estate. The electronically controlled gates were normally closed. A security company vehicle blocked him at the open gate.

Bruce Briggs standing under bright security lights beyond the gate waved him on.

"Hi, Bruce. I'm sorry about your man's death. Did he have a family?"

"He was a sixty-year-old widower with one adult son in the military. His son's taking it hard. They were close. There are no other relatives in the area. Devon Etheridge was a fine, dedicated parent and security officer. We'll all miss him."

"Do you have more details of the incident? I don't understand this thing unless it has some personal connection to me," Mike said.

"All we know so far, after receiving the alarm our office attempted to contact with someone in the house by calling your landline. No one answered. Not waiting, our security captain on duty sent the closest available man to investigate and notified the local police. I wasn't aware of it when we last spoke, but our man arrived and made his way around to the rear of the house within seven minutes of receiving the break-in signal. He reported to the captain that a definite break-in had occurred and was waiting outside for backup. He reported that someone had used a decorative stone from the flower garden to destroy all the glass on the west patio."

Mike drove along the asphalt driveway to a circular turn-around near the house. He parked the Land Rover behind a sheriff's van and two black unmarked vehicles. A uniformed officer met him at the iron gate.

"I'm McGowin, Officer. What's going on here?"

"Investigator Foshee is waiting for you on the west patio, Mr McGowin. He'll talk with you there."

Mike walked along the old brick path around the two-story home to a west side entrance and patio.

Homicide investigator Tony Foshee stepped off the patio.

The two shook hands warmly, having met before at community civic functions on several occasions.

"Hi, Mike. I'm terribly sorry for what's happened here. Let's start outside where the homicide took place." Tony walked to a corner of the patio, taking a position there. "The security officer stood right about here, well back from the damaged entrance to the house. He was concentrating on the point of entry when his attacker approached from behind and stabbed him in the right side of his neck. The knife severed the right carotid artery. Another, unnecessary wound was administered as a deep stab wound to the throat just above the breastbone. The puzzling part, the murder weapon was left to be found near the victim."

"May I see the knife?" Mike said. "Tony, this may be personally connected to me. It may be a message or warning. There's no other reason for this kind of killing."

They entered the house, through the open wall where the glass had been. Tony pointed. "That heavy stone was picked up and thrown several times until all six wide panels extending the length of the patio were demolished." He picked up a clear plastic bag containing the knife from a decorative table. "This thing lends itself toward something a man might carry as a personal weapon, maybe a professional."

Mike held the bag for a moment before handing it back. Adrenalin flooded through his veins. He had seen that knife. No, not that one. One like it. He recognized the heavy folding knife as the type taken weeks earlier from the late Lance Howell.

"Tony, we need to make ourselves comfortable for a few minutes while I tell you a horrible story relating to a knife very much like this one. But first. Was there any additional damage that we should look after?"

"Not that we can find. You may see things different."

"If it isn't evident to you, Tony, I doubt there'd be anything significant. Let's sit here and go over what I know and what I fear may be going on here. I've been out of the country for the last six weeks. The maid and our other service people are the only ones who should've been on the property during that time. I don't believe any of those people can be connected to this incident. Before I leave here today, I'll provide you with important contact information at FBI Headquarters in Washington, DC. The agent in charge of a recently completed major operation here on the west coast was Assistant Director Max Findley. I'll advise him or his staff to expect your call. I'm baffled by what's happened here. It's quite possibly connected to recent drug enforcement and FBI arrests here in California. Now, let me tell you what I know."

Mike told the story of another knife like the one held in evidence. He included a short narrative of the drug operation, and his own unfortunate participation. He gave a statement, finished with the local investigators, and returned to talk more with head of security, Briggs. He arranged to have armed guards posted at his home on an around the clock basis. Mike looked at his watch, saw it was almost three a.m. He felt restless, needing time to think.

Something bothered him. His father's collection of classic automobiles may have been targeted. He entered a service closet from the kitchen and picked out a labeled set of keys. He threw several electrical switches and exited the kitchen through a well-maintained garden, near the illuminated pool area. He waved to one of the armed security guards, checked in with him.

"Hello, Officer. Anything else unusual around here this morning?"

"Not that I'm aware of, sir. Can I help you with something?"

"I'm going to be looking over the outlying area and the automobile storage house. Keep an eye on me, please. I may need you."

He left the pool patio, walked down the long lighted path to the vehicle storage area below the swimming pool. He intended to look over the classic cars stored with his mother's Mercedes, convinced someone familiar with the late Lance Howell and his obsession for revenge had taken over the vendetta. *Can't discount the danger to myself or my new family. The events this evening are personal. Better stay aware here. Why no mention made of the valuable classic automobiles stored below in the auto warehouse?* Had the local police and security patrol failed to inspect this corner of the property following the break-in? It would be unusual for anyone seeing the auto collection to avoid commenting. He hoped he was wrong.

Mike approached the array of automatic doors with the electronic control on a lanyard around his neck. He decided to check out the small entrance doors on each side of the building first, lightweight doors being a likely entry point for vandals planning to do damage to valuables stored inside. He walked to the left side first. The overhead security light was out. Without hesitating, he turned and walked back toward the pool where the security guard was keeping an eye on him.

Mike explained. "The security light is out over the entrance to the auto storage. It makes my antenna quiver a bit. I'd like for you to palm your weapon, hold it close to your thigh and walk back with me. We'll see what's going on, if anything."

Mike opened his fly, pulled out his own weapon, turned, held the weapon close, and walked back down the path. The guard followed a short distance away. They passed near a small avocado tree on Mike's left, moving toward the darkened door, both men cautious. The guard stared at the darkened door, stepping close to a larger tree near the parking lot.

A dark figure dropped from the tree, knocked him to the hard surface. His hand-gun skidded away into the dark shadows. Mike watched the scuffle. He remained unmoving with the Sig held tight against his right leg.

The heavy figure in dark clothing spoke to the guard. "Stay down and you'll live."

Mike elected to stand steady unless the guard was threatened further. He studied the attacker from ten feet away, in poor light, unsure. Recognition hit him like a falling tree.

Lance Howell glared back at him through a mask of hate. "No man ever laid a hand on me and lived! You thought you'd gotten away with it, didn't you? I've lost everything because of your big ass meddling in my business. You killed my damn brother. I want you to know it's your time to die, a thousand small cuts. The pain won't stop until I'm ready to end it."

Mike eased forward. "I don't know how in hell you arranged this amazing resurrection, woman beater. It's more than likely short-lived."

Lance ran directly at Mike, with knife pointing at his stomach.

Mike raised the weapon in one smooth motion, fired twice. Both bullets struck center mass.

He saw the soft hollow point projectiles penetrate the dark clothing barely left of center. He watched the man fall. He switched his eyes to the security guard from the black clad figure, then back again, before replacing the weapon in his pocket. He carefully lifted the injured guard to his feet, then looked at the dark clad figure again before moving into the darkness to look for the gun dropped by the guard. Certain the assailant was down, he moved farther into the shadows looking for the lost weapon.

Lance Howell got his breath back, ran a hand under the bullet proof vest to massage his bruised chest. He saw Mike and the guard moving around in the dark, grabbed the opportunity, crawled ten feet to a thick hedge, and burrowed himself into the shadow of low hanging limbs.

Mike looked back. "Son-of-a-bitch has pulled another Houdini act. Quick! Look behind the hedge row while I check the tree. He can't be far away."

The guard rushed back around the hedge. "He's not behind the shrubbery, must be in the tree." He turned on a small MAG light directing it into the tree.

Mike grabbed the light, directed it around the perimeter then back into the tree. He walked all around. "The tree's empty. The bastard had a vest on for protection. Be careful, he's full of tricks." He placed the Sig in his belt. "Let's check the hedge again. Direct your light at the shadow along the bottom. I'll take one side, you take the other. Don't get close enough to the hedge for another attack. You won't be that lucky again."

From his side of the hedge Mike could see the light shining through the thin growth at the bottom, removing the dark shadow. "Stop!" He yelled. "Move your light back along the bottom again."

Mike pulled his weapon from his belt, backing up several feet. "Come out of the hedge, Lance. The vest won't save you this time."

Lance squirmed out from under the low hanging branches. He gained one knee, hesitated a moment and then sprang at Mike, with another knife in hand.

Mike stepped aside, fired two quick head shots from close range. He followed up with two more to the groin area, below the vest. The first soft hollow point lifted a section of scalp, the second entered one eye, blowing brain matter out above one ear. "Now, try coming back from that you murdering bastard. I just introduced you to the devil." *You don't carry a knife to a gun fight.*

"I thought this damn night would never end, Tony." Mike picked up the fresh brewed pot of coffee, poured three cups and passed them around. Investigator Tony Foshee passed one cup on to the bruised-up security guard. The three men had gathered in Mike's kitchen after detectives had left.

His call to Washington earlier had stimulated abnormal action in the local FBI Office. Agents familiar with Task Force Able activated an emergency protocol, drawing in representatives from local, state and federal law enforcement agencies. Agents were ordered to appear at the crime scene for a special, on-scene briefing immediately. Drug enforcement connected the killing of drug lord Lance Howell to several local killings related to larger ongoing operations. Thus, the noisy crowd assembled earlier in Mike's main dining room. The noisy meeting ended without fanfare. Howell was declared dead at the scene.

Bruce Briggs, president of Briggs Security and Investigations, joined Mike in the spacious kitchen.

"Thanks for bringing in the two very efficient women on short notice for kitchen service, Bruce. The fresh gee-dunks were the hit of the evening."

The women had brought in several dozen fresh pastries to supplement coffee for the meeting with gathered law enforcement officers.

Bruce asked, "Did you ever find out who this guy was, Mike?"

"Oh yeah! The FBI had been puzzling over records of Lance Howell and a Larry Howell, both showing the same year of birth. Up to now, the FBI thought they were one and the same person. As it turned out, they were both born in San Bernardino, less than one year apart, were brothers. As children, they moved to Cabo San Lucas, Mexico with their mother and did not return to the United States until they were teenagers. Larry had an extensive arrest record. He'd been running a drug distribution network in the Inland Empire. He seldom traveled to Mexico. The two interacted mainly with Lance in the States."

Chapter 35

Max Findley stepped down from the helicopter onto the ships deck. *Woah, this damn thing's still moving.*

Coast Guard Commander Cheyne Douglas ducked low against the rotor wash, grabbed an elbow and led Max away from the spinning helicopter rotors. "Welcome aboard US Coast Guard Ship *Adak*, sir. We've been expecting you. He pointed above. "Better watch your head through these low passage-ways, sir. Agent in charge, Parkhill of DEA and Homeland Security representative Mr James Bailey are waiting in the ward-room, sir."

The ward-room on the Coast Guard ship looked small to Max. DEA Agent Parkhill grabbed his hand. "Thank you, Max, for the excellent job you've done getting us to this point. The overall combined operation made a hell of a dent in the volume of illegal drugs entering the country from Mexico. I believe you know Jim Bailey."

"Yes! Hi, Jim, good to see you."

"Well, gentlemen. Things are coming together the way we hoped. Our people on the scene in Mexico sent word this afternoon that Howell's man, Palmyra, made a new delivery at two p.m. Any sooner and we wouldn't have had assets in place for the take down."

Parkhill looked directly at Max. "You were successful keeping the Catalina Island action out of the news or we wouldn't be here so soon."

Jim Bailey said, "Yes. About that, Max. Your agents must have laughed their asses off after hearing the rumor coming up from the low-level drug community about Howell's disappearing act. They're saying he took off with his big yacht before cartel discipline caught up with him. Some say he disappeared at the hands of drug lord Federico Quanta."

"Yeah, for now. It's just a matter of time before word filters back to the cartel through Mexican law enforcement. They're bonded at the hip."

Commander Douglas stuck his head in the door. "There's an urgent up-date for you Agent Parkhill, from Coast Guard air. The freighter *San Delphino* entered international waters an hour ago. They picked up our vessels on radar and slowed to a crawl."

Parkhill turned to Cheney. "Activate boarding orders at once, Commander. They probably got word about the Port San Quinten raid through Mexican Drug enforcement." He looked at Max. "I guess you're right. Let's get those container numbers to the boarding party right away."

Jim Bailey said, "That's damn fast information from our agents with the Mexican authorities. A smart move, getting specific container information from arrested crews returning to San Quintin. Must have offered cash incentives and maybe reduced charges."

"Most likely," Parkhill said. "Just the kind of specific information we need. Won't have to open up every damn container on board to get the critical evidence. We also have an update on the raid, gentlemen.

"The operation proved successful beyond expectations. Already, stand-by agents have arrested six major distributors from California, Oregon, and Washington. Listen to this. Thirteen major dealers operating in major cities between the Mexican border and Canadian border have also been apprehended, with more arrests to be made."

Jim Bailey said. "That's great news, Chuck. Now let's get the shippers in the net."

Commander Douglas looked up from the computer screen. "Visual aid is now hooked up to the Special Ops boarding party, gentlemen. Ops personnel rappelled down from helicopters. They landed without opposition.

"Container ship *San Delphino* is dead in the water. DEA inspectors are now boarding from small craft. We now have big screen capability. Just sit back and watch the show, gentlemen."

Ninety minutes later, James Bailey from Homeland Security turned off his recorder. "That's the damnedest thing I've ever seen. That ship had seven identified containers on board, thanks to those recorded numbers. Each container carried at least two small boats loaded with contraband of one kind or another. I congratulate the task force and all of you involved in this well-run operation. Max, your agents are going to be busy for a while longer running down stragglers."

Jim Bailey tapped Max on the shoulder. "So, you and Chuck are heading out to board *San Delphino* for the wrap up. That should be interesting."

"There's an old saying in the military, Jim. 'No job's done until the paperwork's finished.' The real wrap up starts then, back in Washington."

Jim Bailey reached across the table to shake hands. "Thank you, gentlemen, for keeping us informed. Good luck boarding that ship."

Chapter 36

Mike drove through the parking garage to park behind the guest house. The place looked quiet. He noticed the small electric harbor boat missing from its customary tie down. He crossed the yard, through the large kitchen, into Barbara Blair's personal office. He found Barbara deeply engrossed in reading from a large cookbook. She looked at him.

"You rascal! Stop scaring the dickens out of me. You look tired as hell, Mike. Are you okay?"

"I'm tired but feel great otherwise. Where is everyone? Much too quiet around here."

"The kids all went to the beach. The ladies wanted to shop at the mall, and your dad took all the men for a harbor cruise. Why don't you take advantage of the quiet and go straight up for a rest? By the way, thanks for the phone call. You set everyone's mind at ease."

"Daddy? Wake up. Mom and me. We've been worried about you!"

Mike opened one eye. He squinted into a gorgeous set of blue eyes and a very pretty face.

"Hi, sweetie! What time is it?"

"Mom said it's time for you to get up. We've missed you so much."

"Okay. Can I have a hug first?"

Catherine kissed him on the cheek. She let him pull her close. "Ouch! Daddy, you need a shave."

He noticed Tracy at the door holding a large cup of coffee. "Do I get a hug too, oh exhausted one?"

"For that big cup of coffee, you get two hugs."

Mike finished breakfast and pushed his chair back from the table. "How'd the last board meeting go, Dad? I think I should check into the office right away. I've been away for over a month. That has me concerned."

"Don't worry about it, Mike. Sally and Gayle have everything on track. However, you might want to inspect some of the contractor's work if you have time. You need not be concerned about the new projects. We can let those run into next year if we have to. Your most important concern now? Your new family. All of us here."

"I'd like Tracy to go with me to the home place afterwards. We can be back in time for the gathering at the club tomorrow. I need to check out a few things and she needs to know what she's getting into."

He caught her eye. "What do you think about you and Catherine accompanying me into Los Angeles today? The two of you can get acquainted with your new home while I drop by the office. Tomorrow, I need to visit a couple of job sites before we return here to Dad's place."

Tracy's mom spoke up. "Why don't you leave Catherine here with us so she can get to know Papa Marcus and Barbara?"

"That'd be nice, Mom! What do you think, Mike?"

"Catherine's so much a part of us, Tracy. I don't think I should leave her that long."

She laughed. "That's too bad, Mike." She looked at her mother. "That's a great idea, Mom." She grinned at Mike. "Catherine will enjoy being here with Mom, Papa and Stef. Playing in the pool will be much more fun than a long ride into LA. Besides. I have some shopping to do. I'm still wearing borrowed clothing! Is that okay?"

Everybody laughed at Tracy. Mike put his arm around her. "That does sound good to me if, Mickey agrees."

Mike and Tracy held eye contact until he winked and picked up keys to the Land Rover.

He left highway 101 south at Las Vergennes Canyon exit, turned south again, then east on Mulholland to a private road.

Tracy stared at the gate blocking the road. "What's this, Mike, your country club?" She squeezed Mike's thigh and laughed.

He pushed a button on the console. A huge iron gate slid open. Moments later a large Tudor style home appeared at the end of the road.

"Mom and Dad built this home when I was about Catherine's age. Mom designed the landscaping. She was working as a landscape architect when they met, bidding on his projects. She found this ten-acre parcel after their wedding, and convinced Dad to work with her in building this place."

"Your mother sounds like a very special person, Mike. I want to know everything about her. How did she die, if I may ask?"

"You would've liked her and she would've been crazy about you. She was always after me to find the right girl to settle down with. She dreamed of a house full of grandchildren to spoil."

He parked at the edge of the circular driveway. "Mom died in sort of a freak accident. She was a horse person. You'll see the stables later. About five years ago, she purchased a beautiful gelding jumper she loved. She rode every single morning. One day while they were riding, a coyote jumped out. The horse reared and took off. Mom was so relaxed, the horse ran right out from underneath her. She fell backward, onto the hard-packed bridal trail. She never regained consciousness."

"Oh my God, Mike. That's horrible."

"It was tragic for all of us. I think it caused more serious damage to Dad. He lost interest in the business, sold the horses and moved to the bay house, as he always called it. Now he just calls it home."

"You must have wonderful memories of growing up here. I can tell, it's more than family loyalty. Do you live here all the time, Mike? Or just visit to recharge your energy level?"

"No! It isn't just that. I love this place and hope you and Catherine will love it too. Oh yes, I had a nice apartment on Pico Boulevard before Mom died. But later I realized how important this place was to me. I couldn't let it become just another piece of property on the real-estate market."

"From what I've seen already, Catherine and I would be out of our minds if we objected to living here with you. Finding you and loving you again is all we require. This will be our home. We'll do our best to make you proud and happy, with maybe just a few minor disappointments from time to time."

She leaned against him, kissing his ear lightly, then slid a hand along his thigh. Her mischievous kisses created havoc with his concentration. After a few moments of passion, they left the Land Rover, breathing hard.

Tracy walked to an old-fashioned split rail fence, covered with ivy. "Oh my God, Mike! It's beautiful!" She pointed to a ten-foot waterfall, flowing over black volcanic rock before dropping another two feet into a crystal-clear swimming pool. "The flora and fauna of this place is spectacular. Would I have to clean the pool? Please tell me you have a crew to manage this amazing property!"

Tracy shifted her attention away from the waterfall. "What's that attractive building with all the big doors, there, down below the pool cabana?"

They walked in that direction, "That's where we park the cars. The Spanish tile area is for extra parking when entertaining."

Tracy stopped in her tracks. "Will you expect me to do a lot of entertaining?"

"No, honey, trust me. You'll make plenty of friends here. That'll be your call, on your terms. I'll be happy if it's our close friends and family. You and Catherine will have years to choose your friends here."

"Mike, I haven't even been in your gorgeous home. Can we go inside now? What an attractive entrance. The classic leaded glass goes well with the home's overall design. So how does this get managed? Who in the world takes care of it?"

"The pool service is weekly. The gardener comes two days a week, a landscaping company comes semi-monthly and the maid would like to come in twice each week. At the present time, her crew is here once a week. You can help me evaluate all these services once you're settled and feel at home. You'll be surprised how fast you adjust to managing the estate, which I'll appreciate. I can concentrate on business. Does it scare you?"

"Not really. In fact, as you explain it. I look forward to sharing the responsibility. I'm overwhelmed at the moment but most importantly, I want to make you happy and proud of me."

"I'm proud of you, sweetheart. I love you like crazy. It feels like no time at all has passed since we took that plunge into the Christmas tree. Are you sure we haven't been together these last ten years? I've never been so comfortable with anyone else in my entire life. I never doubted we were destined for each other."

"So, have I, Mike. I've longed for you, allowed my pride to steal ten years from our lives. I'm so sorry for doing that to you."

Tears welled in her eyes. They held each other close for several long moments, then began moving again, on through the front door.

He walked her through the house. "I'm overwhelmed with this home, beginning to understand your mother and why you couldn't turn your back on this heritage. It's beautiful, yet unique and personal."

They moved into the upstairs rooms. "Every room is large and well furnished with large closets. But why two master bedrooms? Both have floor to ceiling glass overlooking the pool area. I'm certain your parents were devoted lovers, not desiring separate bedrooms."

"You're right about that! Until Mom died this was one large room and very personal. I'll tell you all about it later."

Tracy opened the door to the master bedroom, wandered close to the king-sized bed. She looked up at Mike, turned and pulled the covers back, smiling at Mike. "Do you really need to visit your office today, Mike?"

He put both hands on her soft backside and pulled her tight against him. "Of course not. I'm going crazy, and I want a lot more than a tender kiss after two weeks of close physical contact with the most beautiful girl on the planet."

"I know, Mike! I feel the same way. Let's enjoy each other, our being together. The house is beautiful, but we'll appreciate it more if we finish the tour later. I just want to feel you next to me. I'm not ashamed to admit I've dreamed of having you hold me for years. Please, let's take off our clothes and feel the closeness again."

Mike darkened the room, leaving just enough light to see into each-other's eyes. They removed their clothing one garment at a time, in the soft glow of the recessed lighting until it suddenly wasn't fast enough.

"Do you still love me, Mike? After all this time?"

He cupped her face in his hands. "So much it hurts. I want many more children with you, maybe even a baker's dozen. Think you can handle that?"

"Hell no! But one more might be nice."

Neither could keep their hands off the other. They continued standing, with a hair's distance between the two warm bodies, touching each other with lips and fingertips, bringing up intense sensations and deep emotions. Tracy reached for Mike's hand and dragged him into the turned down bed.

"Hold me, Mike. Hold me so tight it hurts, please, Mike. I want you so much to love me."

Tracy stretched and sat up. "Mike, how long have we been here for gosh sakes? That was a wonderful start to our new life. A rediscovery of myself. I still need you close. Just hold me a while longer."

He put his hand over her mouth to stop her talking. "We now have a lifetime to love each other, sweetheart. Don't you think we should keep practicing until we get it perfect?"

She buried her face against his chest. Tears dampened her cheek, happy tears. "I'm sorry, Mike. You're the only man who ever made me cry." She raised her head, looking into his eyes.

"I've been thinking. We'll never let life get in the way of our happiness again."

Jerry Baggett is a longtime Los Angeles business man and Southern California yachtsman. Jerry grew up on Cape Hatteras Island and the Gulf Coast of Alabama where he developed a love for the sea. After graduating from the University of Alabama, he found his way to Los Angeles where he spent his time between various business interests and love for cruising and diving California's ever-fascinating Channel Islands with his family.

Epilogue

The first week of August, Joel Santiago and the Conwell sisters, each in turn, received a knock at the door. The well-dressed man flashed his identification.

"I'm Agent Stevenson from the Washington office of the Federal Bureau of Investigation. May I see some identification please?

Once identified, each person received a sealed envelope marked PERSONAL. The return address, Internal Revenue Service, Washington D.C.

Later in August 2020, Mike McGowin received a short text message from Max Findley:

'The Eagle has delivered. You owe me.'